COLLECT THE SET!

Boffin Boy and the Invaders from Space
1 84167 613 6

Boffin Boy and the Wizard of Edo
1 84167 614 4

Boffin Boy and the Monsters from the Deep
1 84167 615 2

Boffin Boy and the Red Wolf
1 84167 616 0

Boffin Boy and the Lost City
1 84167 617 9

Boffin Boy and the Time Warriors
1 84167 622 5

Boffin Boy and the Invaders from Space
by David Orme

Illustrated by Peter Richardson

Published by Ransom Publishing Ltd.
Rose Cottage, Howe Hill, Watlington, Oxon. OX49 5HB
www.ransom.co.uk

ISBN   184167 613 6
        978 184167 613 5
First published in 2006

A CIP catalogue record of this book is available from the British Library.

Design & layout: *www.macwiz.co.uk*

Find out more about Boffin Boy at *www.ransom.co.uk*.

Boffin Boy
AND THE
Invaders
from Space

By David Orme
Illustrated by Peter Richardson

Ransom

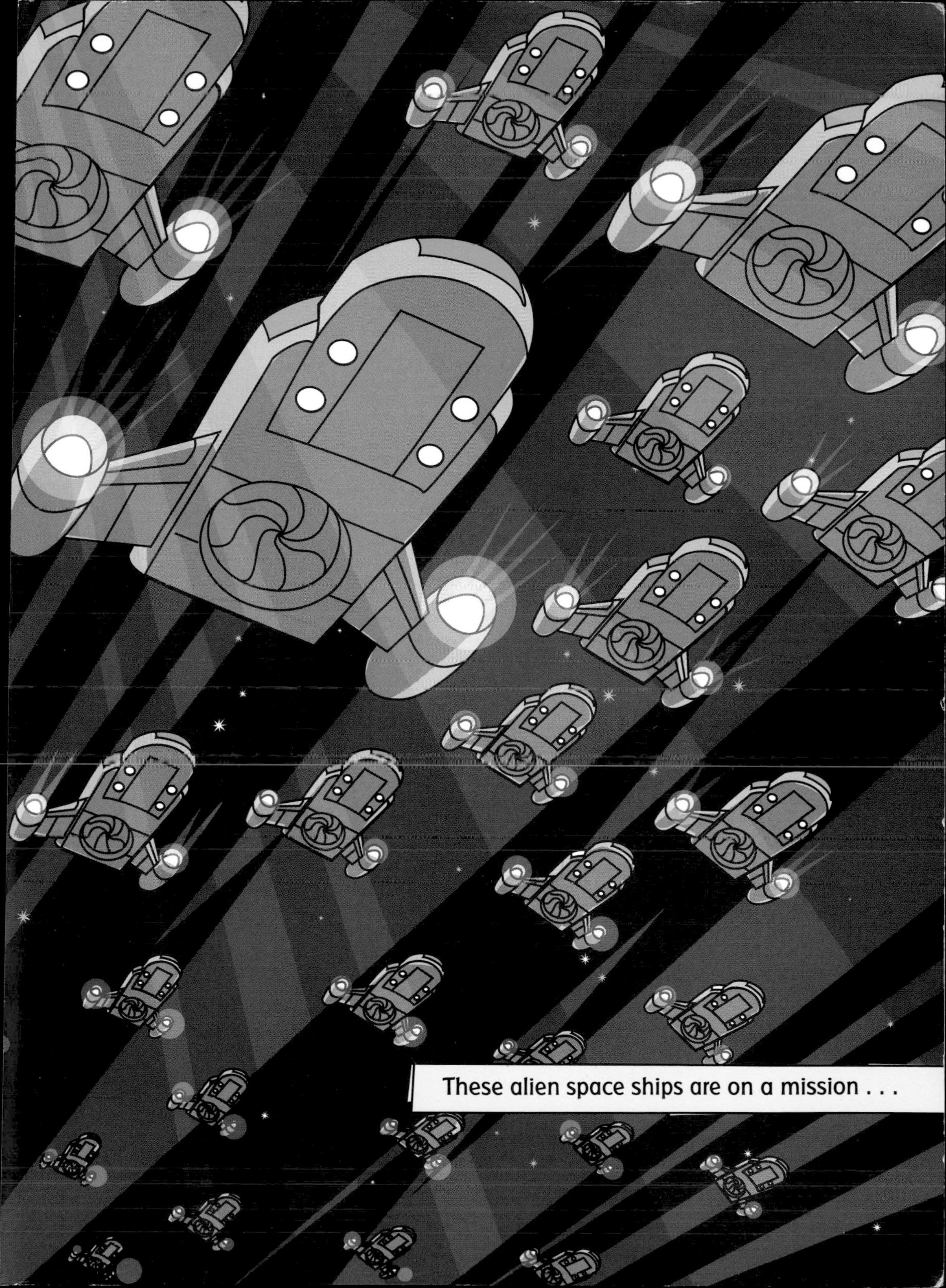
These alien space ships are on a mission . . .

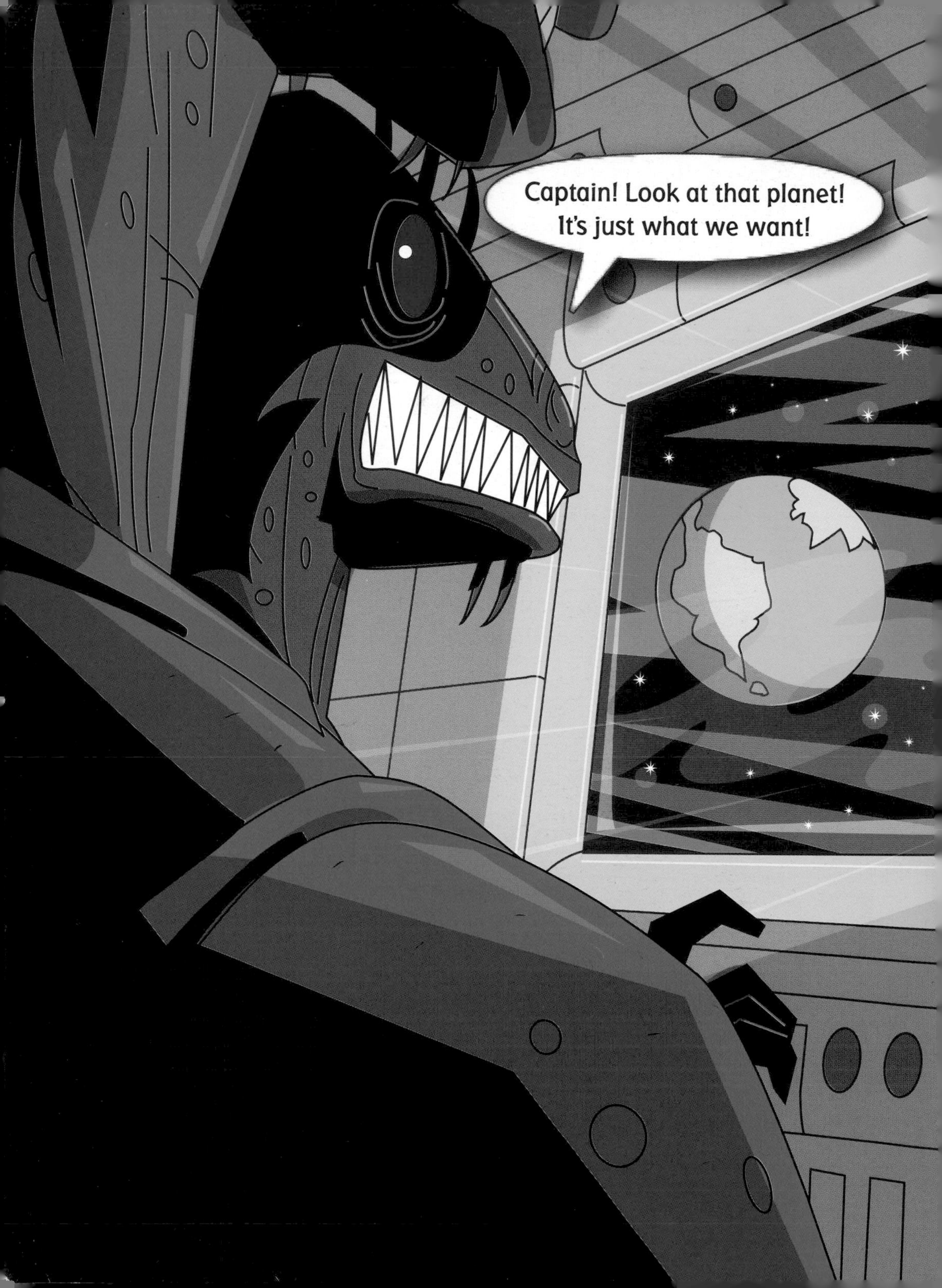
Captain! Look at that planet! It's just what we want!

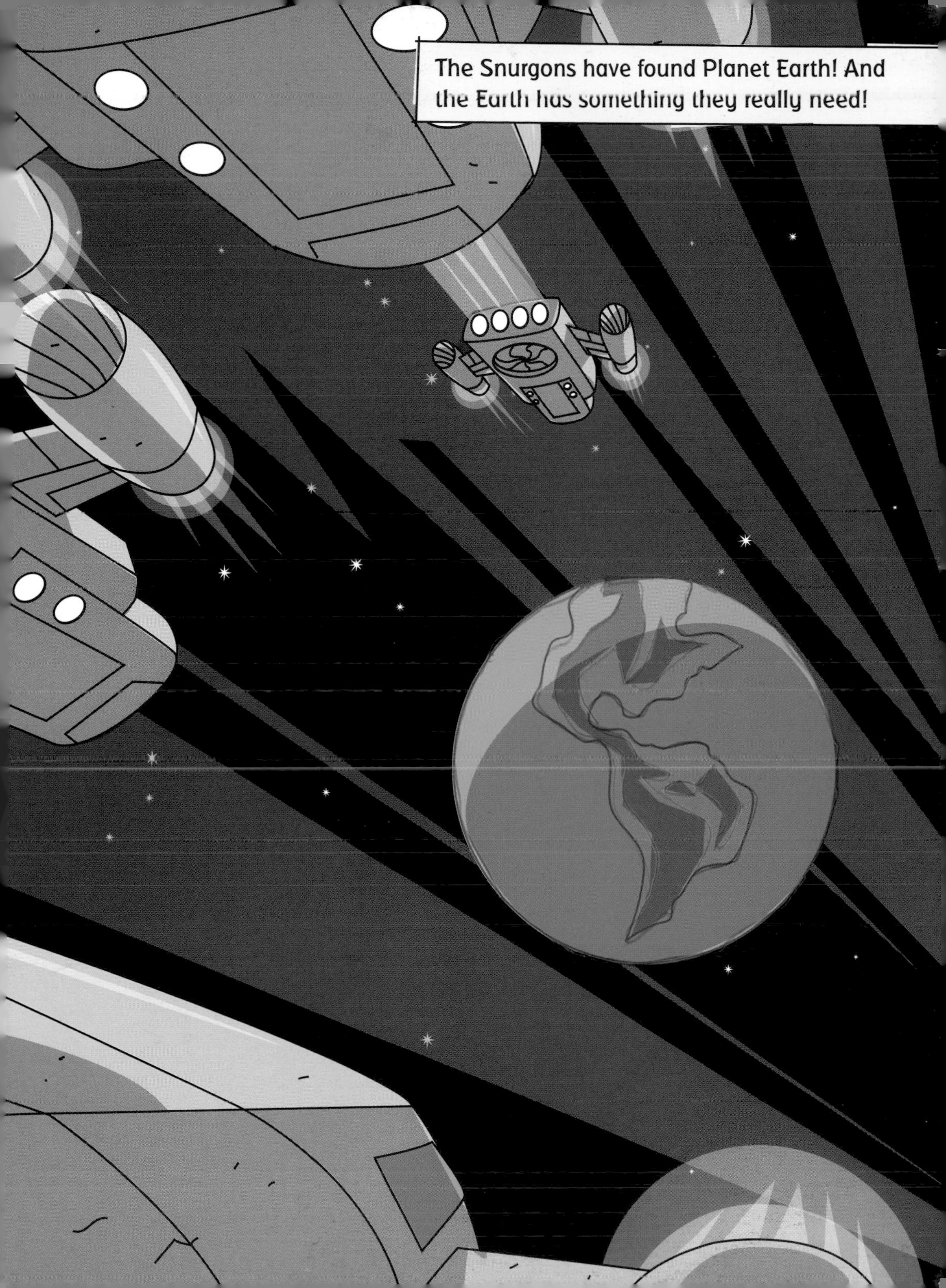
The Snurgons have found Planet Earth! And the Earth has something they really need!

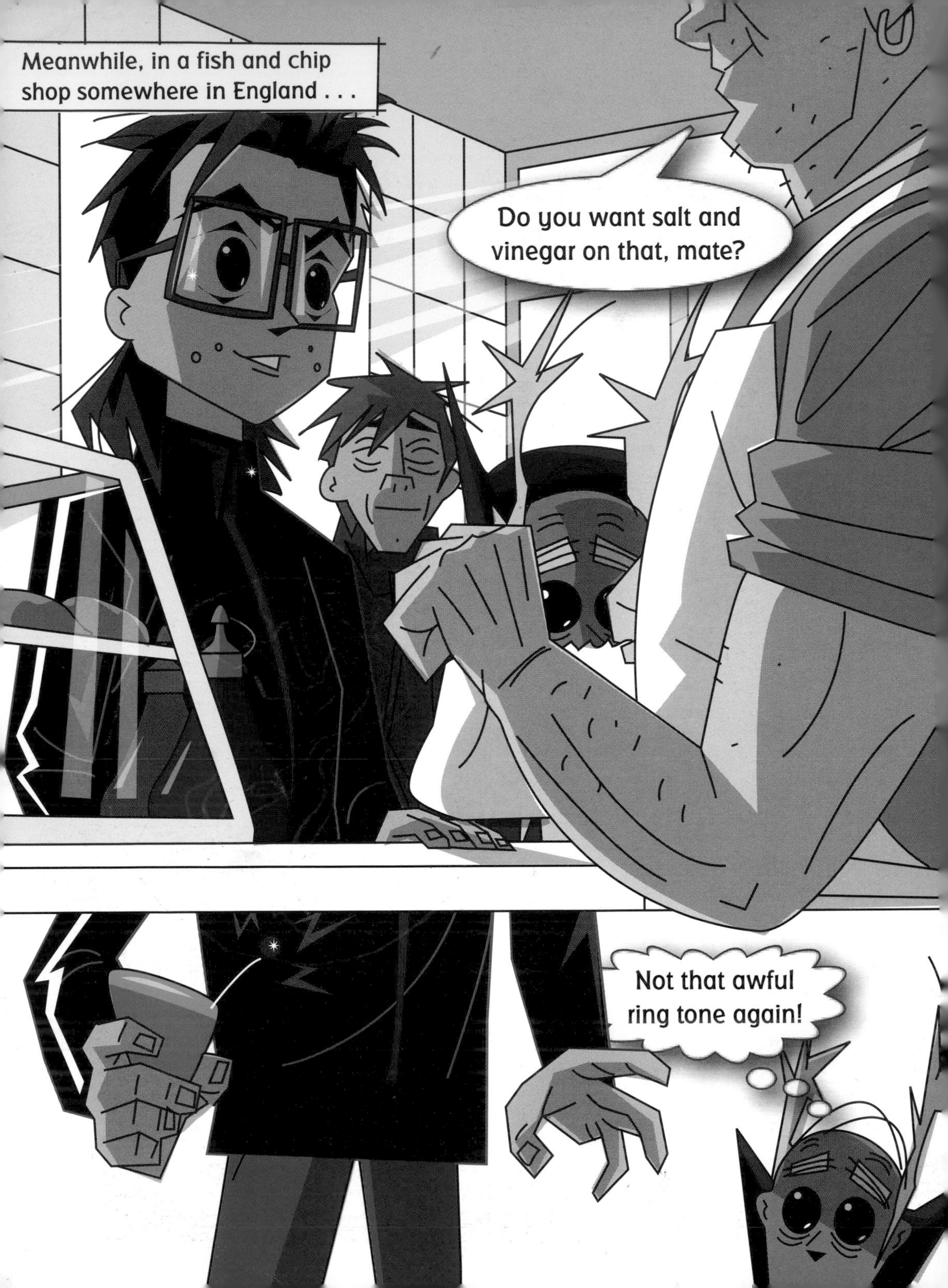
Meanwhile, in a fish and chip shop somewhere in England . . .
Do you want salt and vinegar on that, mate?
Not that awful ring tone again!

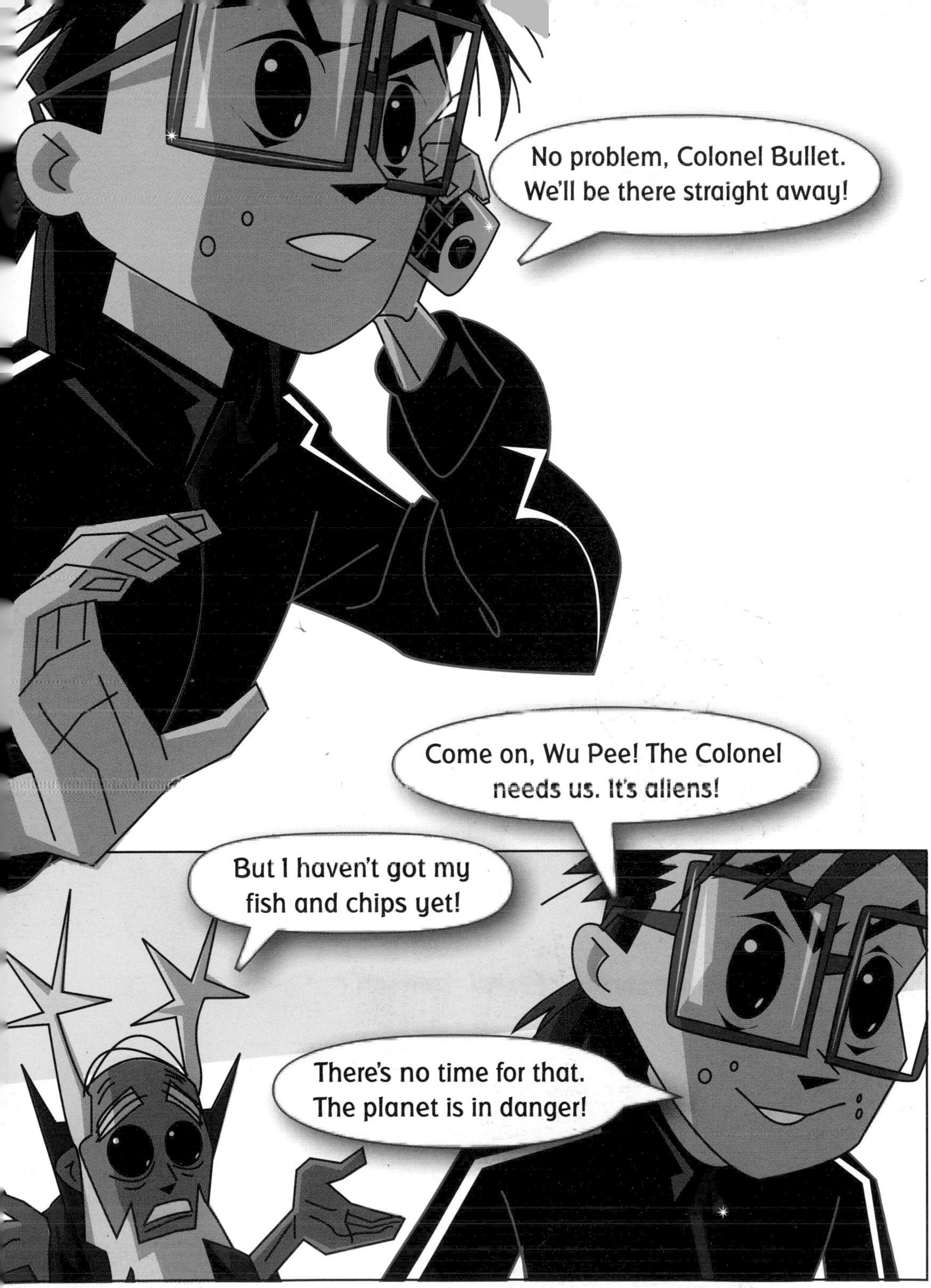
No problem, Colonel Bullet. We'll be there straight away!
Come on, Wu Pee! The Colonel needs us. It's aliens!
But I haven't got my fish and chips yet!
There's no time for that. The planet is in danger!

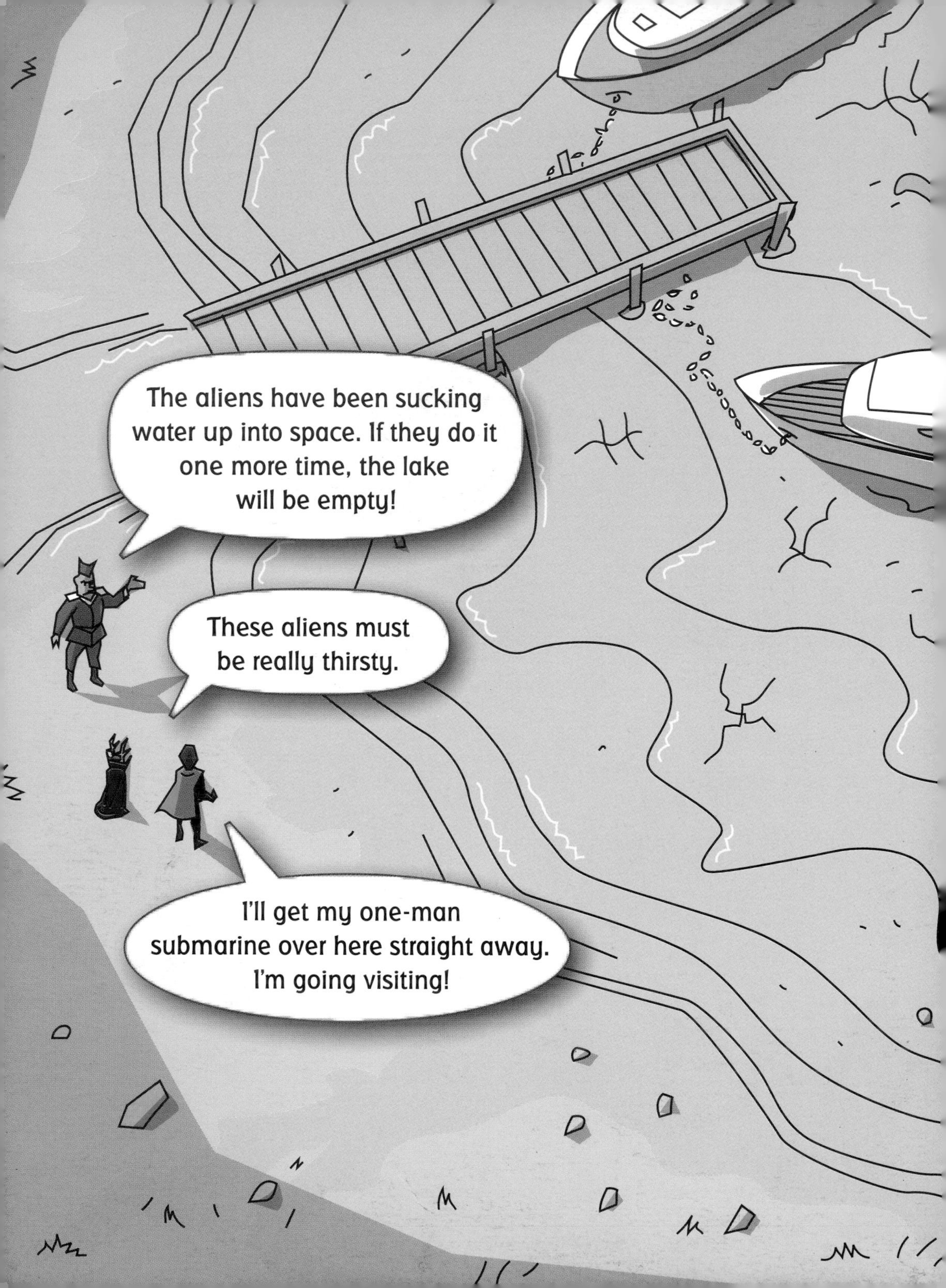
The aliens have been sucking water up into space. If they do it one more time, the lake will be empty!
These aliens must be really thirsty.
I'll get my one-man submarine over here straight away. I'm going visiting!

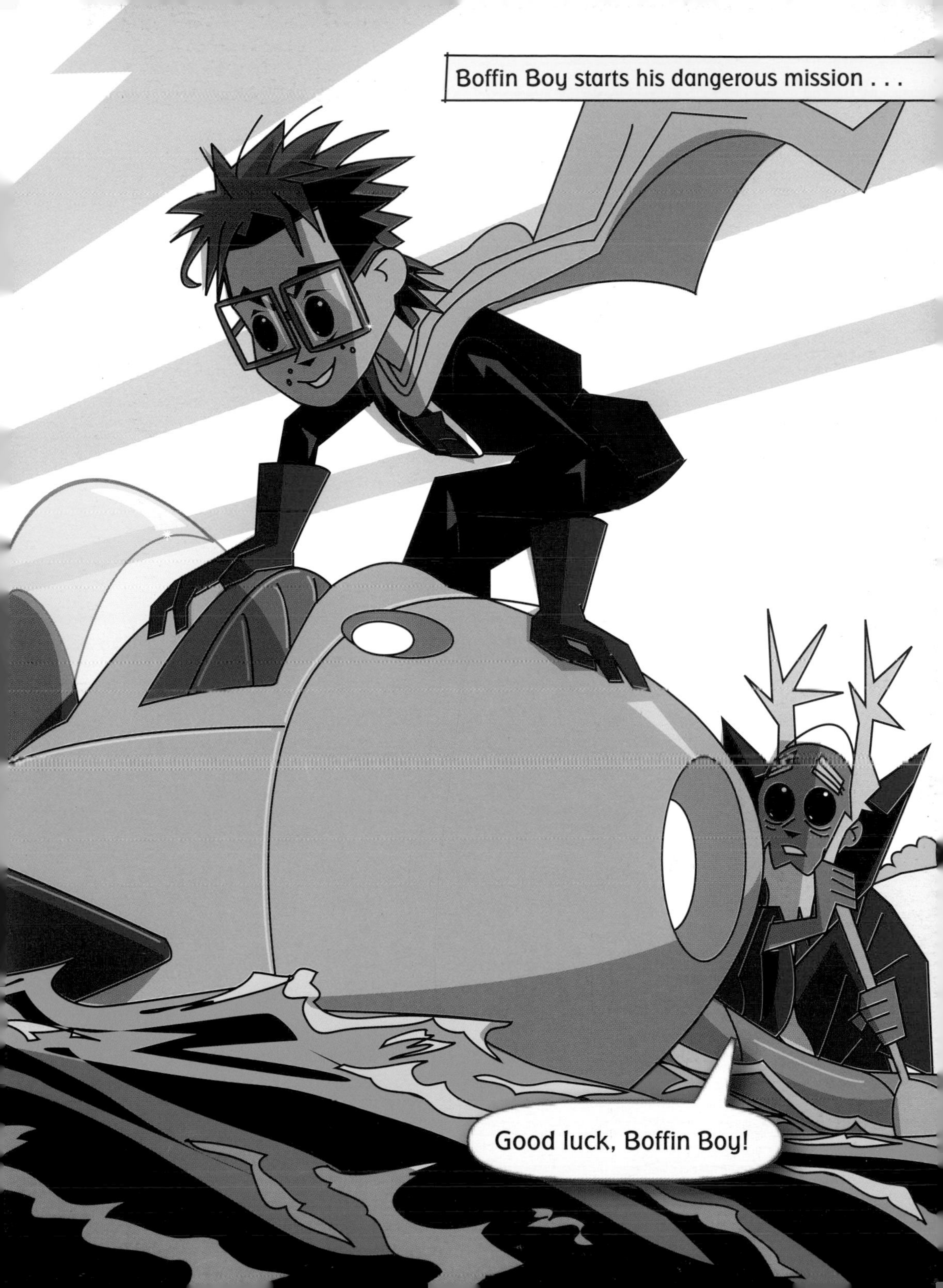
Boffin Boy starts his dangerous mission . . .
Good luck, Boffin Boy!

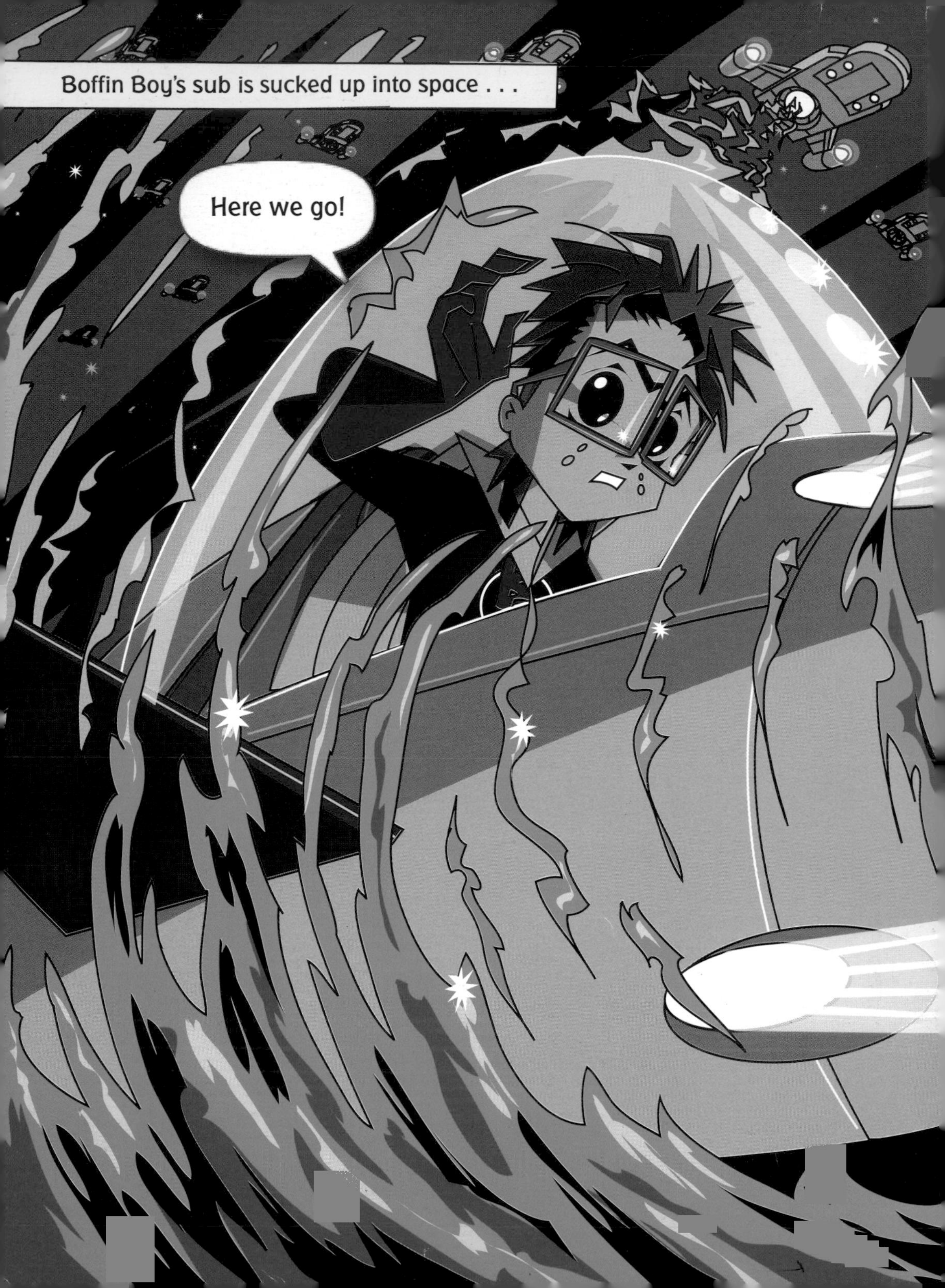
Boffin Boy's sub is sucked up into space . . .
Here we go!

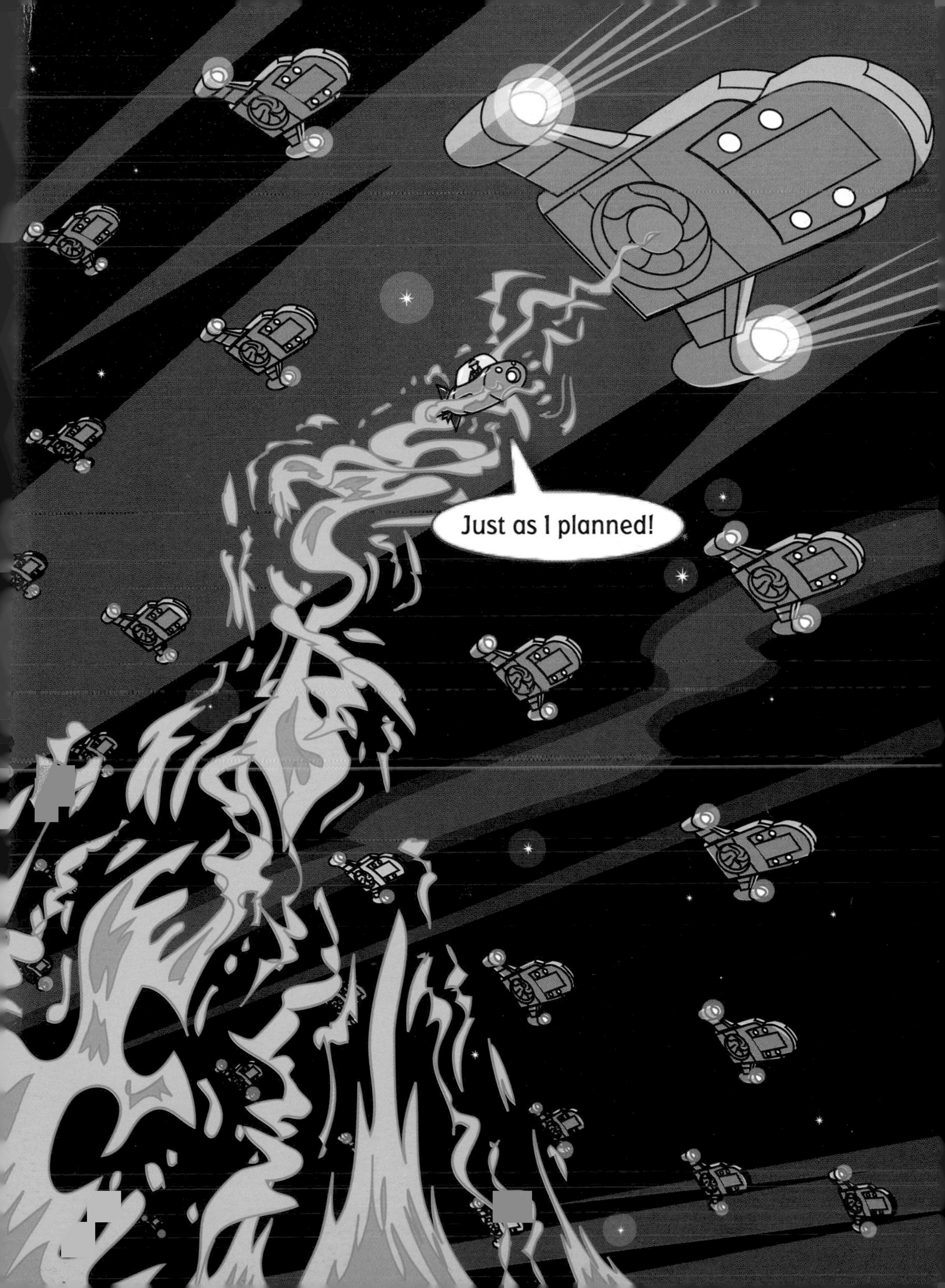
Just as I planned!

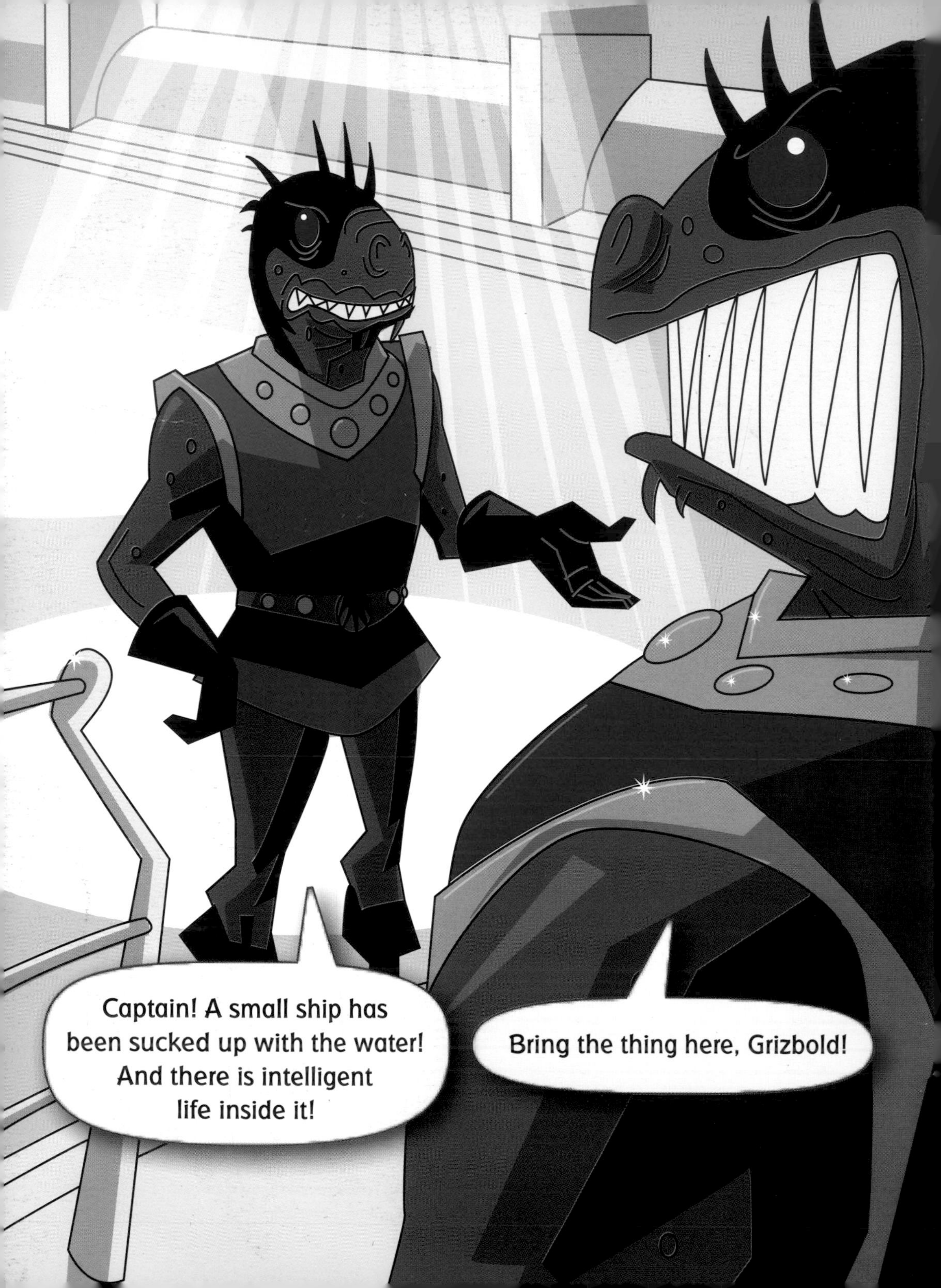
Captain! A small ship has been sucked up with the water! And there is intelligent life inside it!
Bring the thing here, Grizbold!

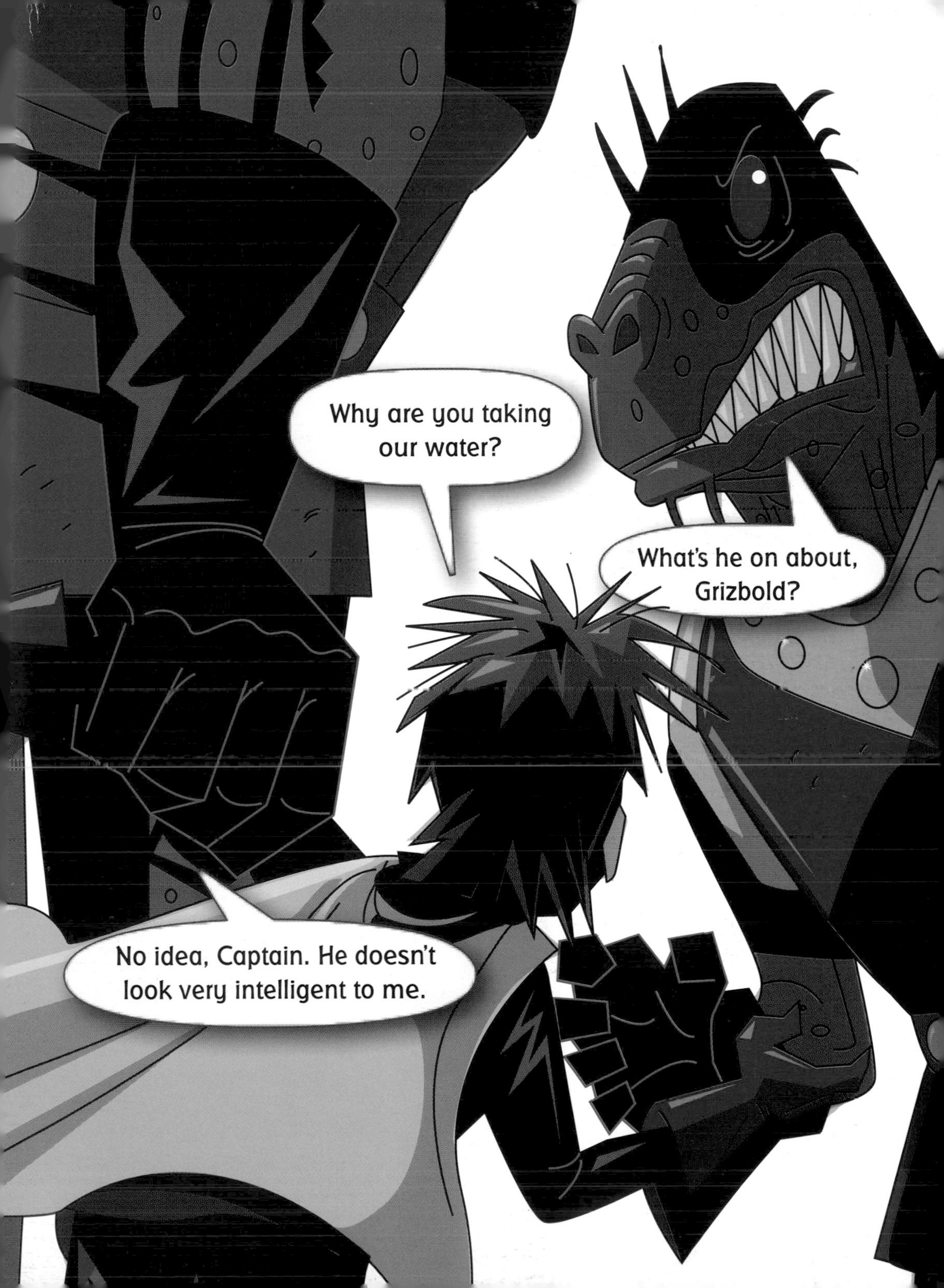
Why are you taking our water?
What's he on about, Grizbold?
No idea, Captain. He doesn't look very intelligent to me.

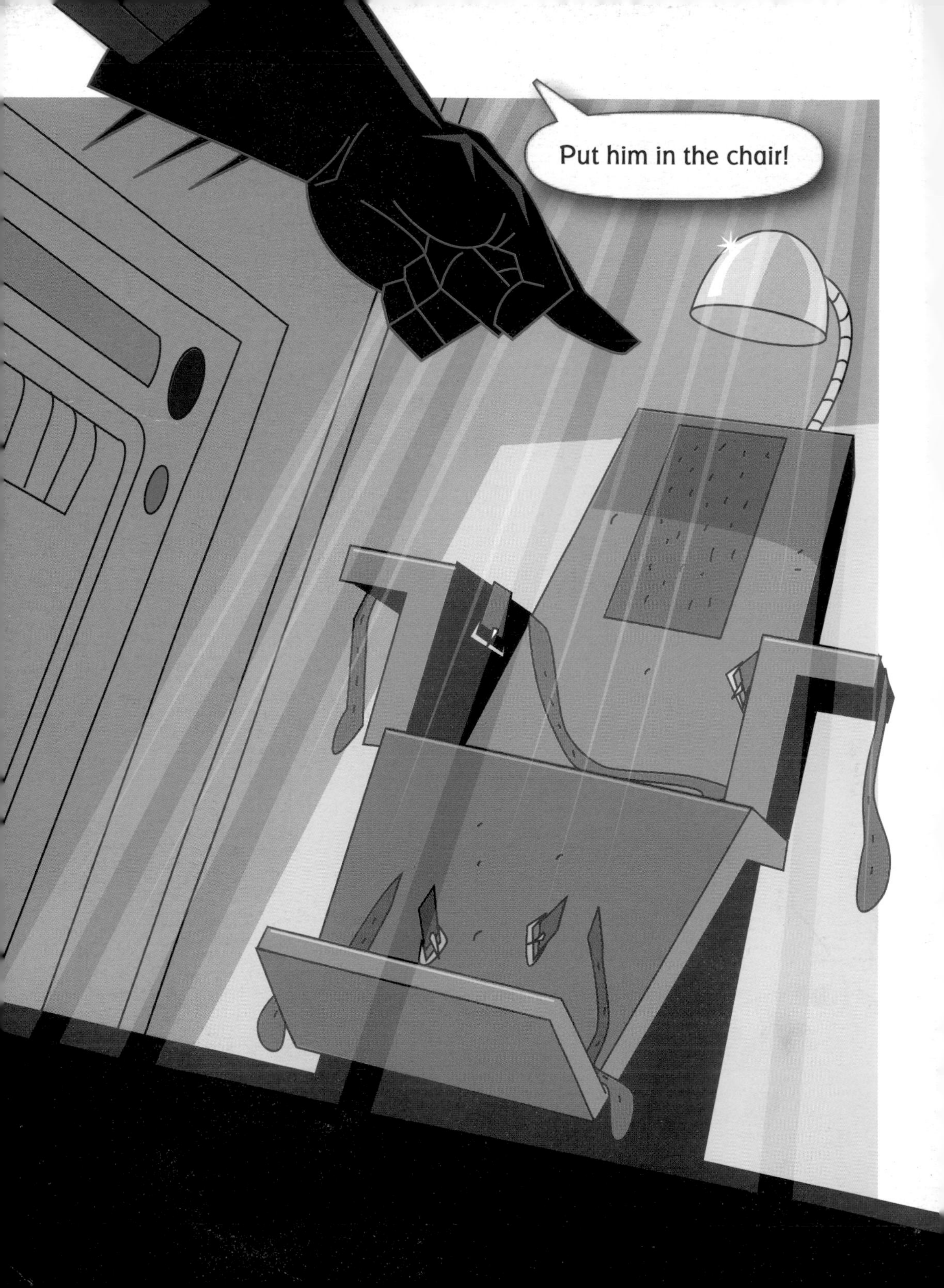
Put him in the chair!

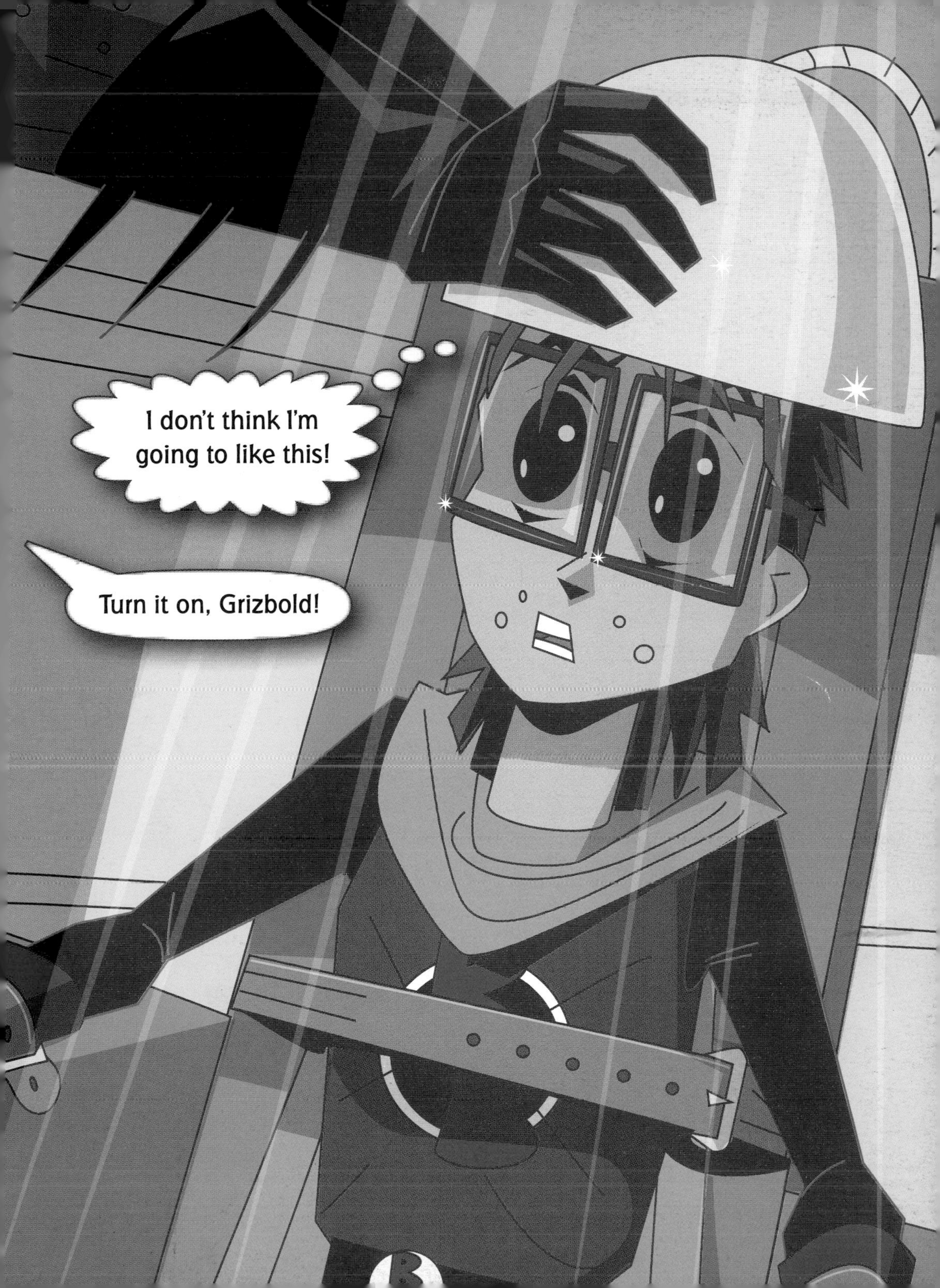
I don't think I'm going to like this!
Turn it on, Grizbold!

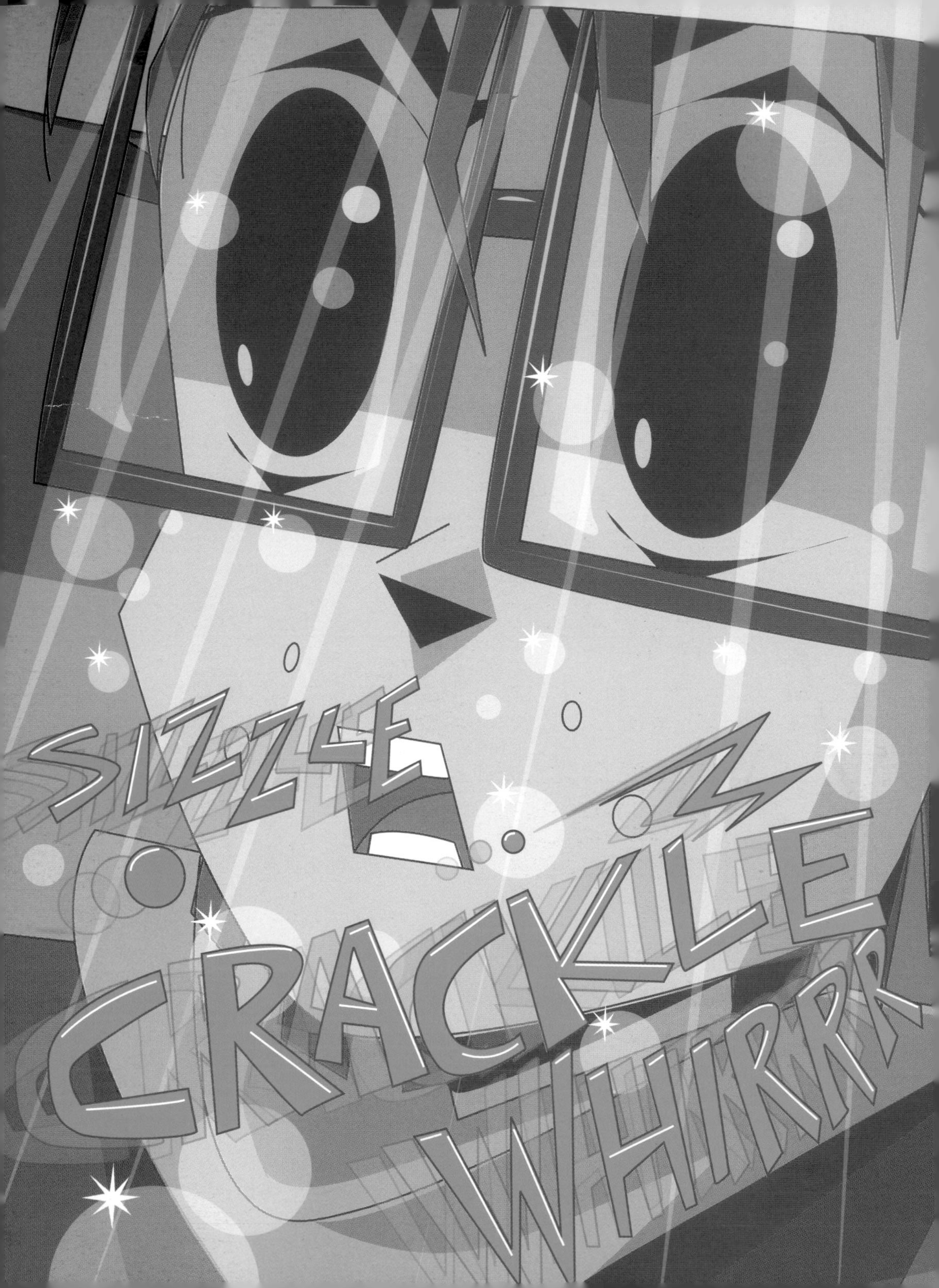
SIZZLE
CRACKLE
WHIRRR

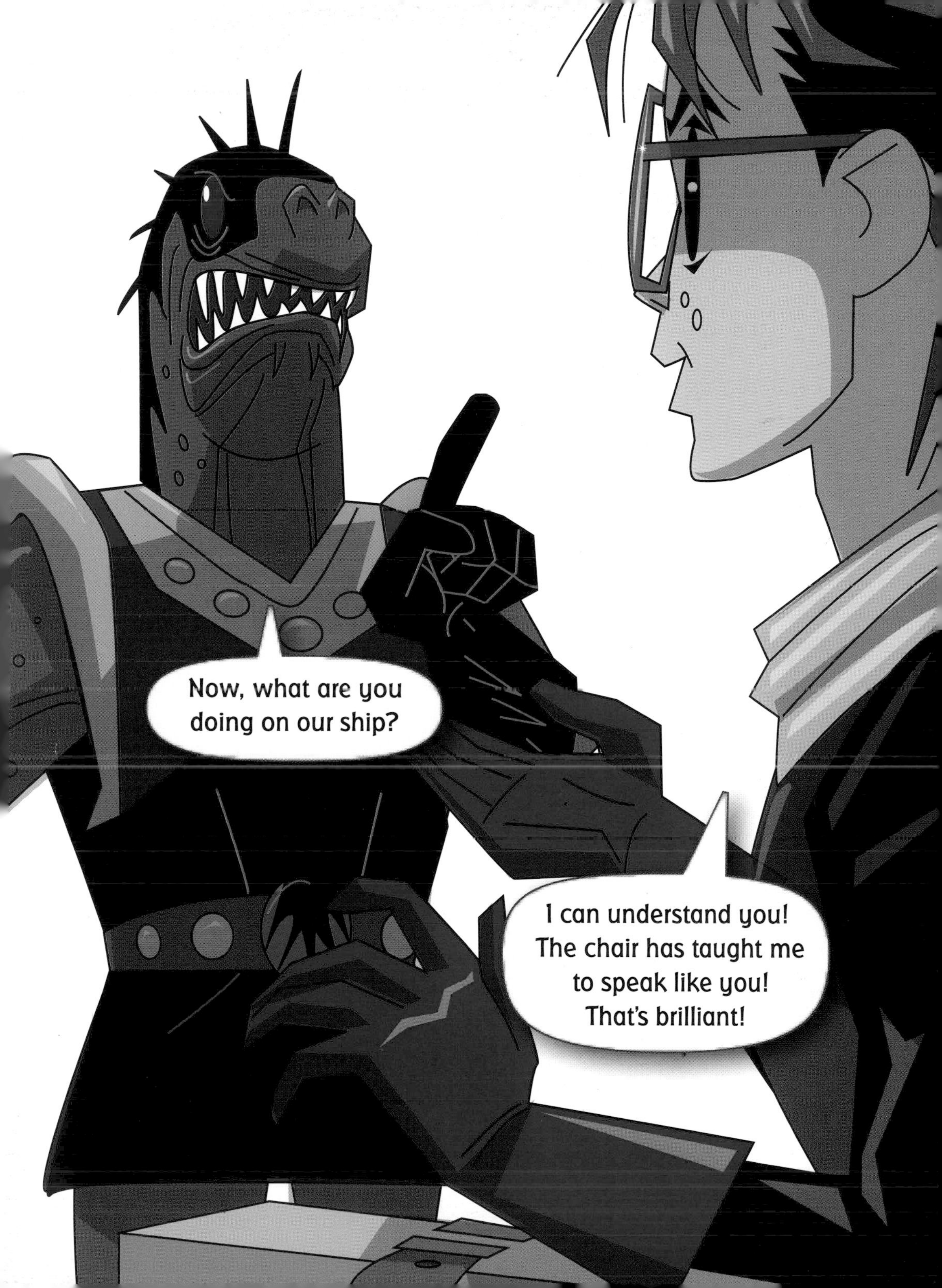
Now, what are you doing on our ship?
I can understand you! The chair has taught me to speak like you! That's brilliant!

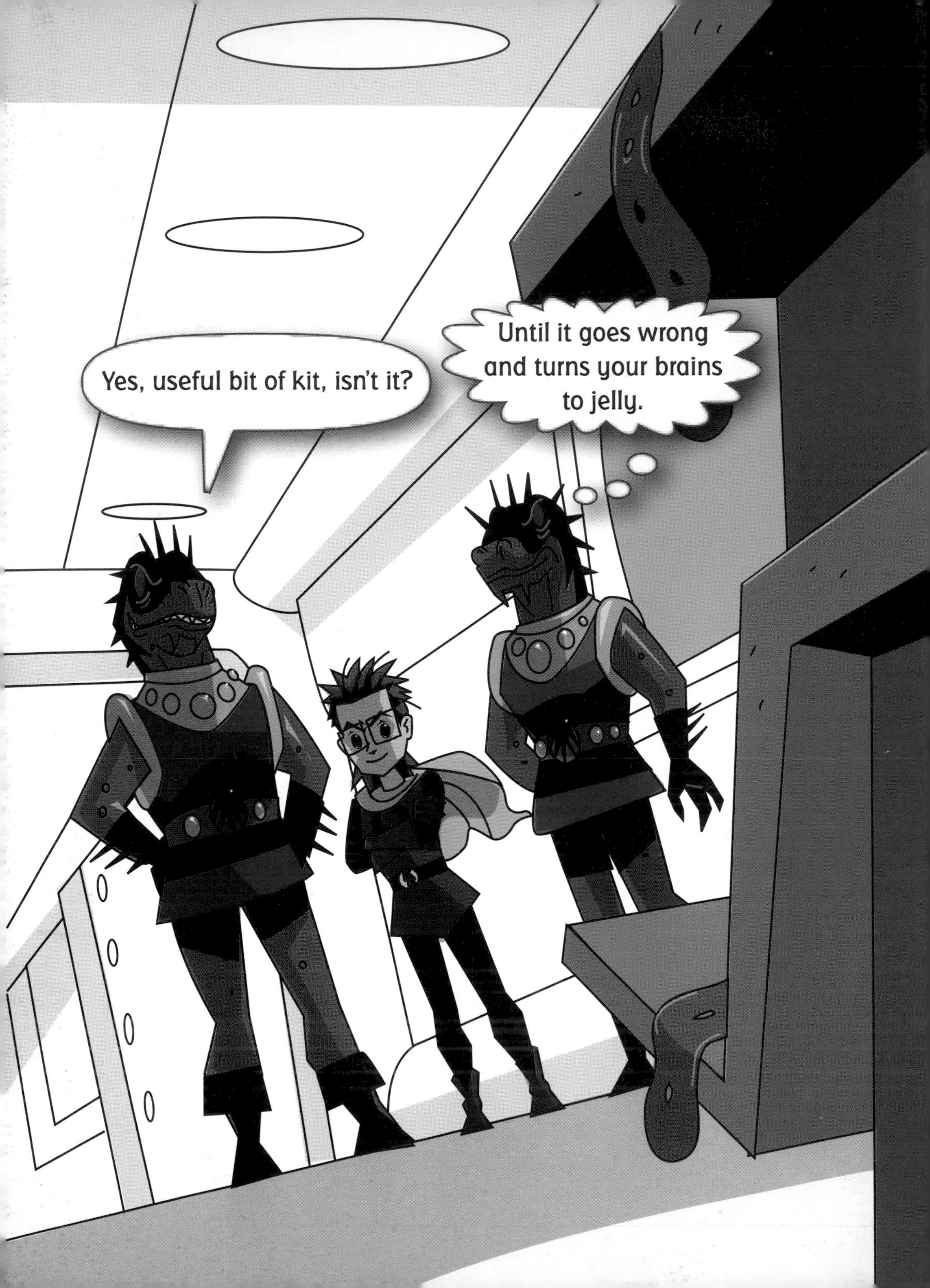
Yes, useful bit of kit, isn't it?
Until it goes wrong and turns your brains to jelly.

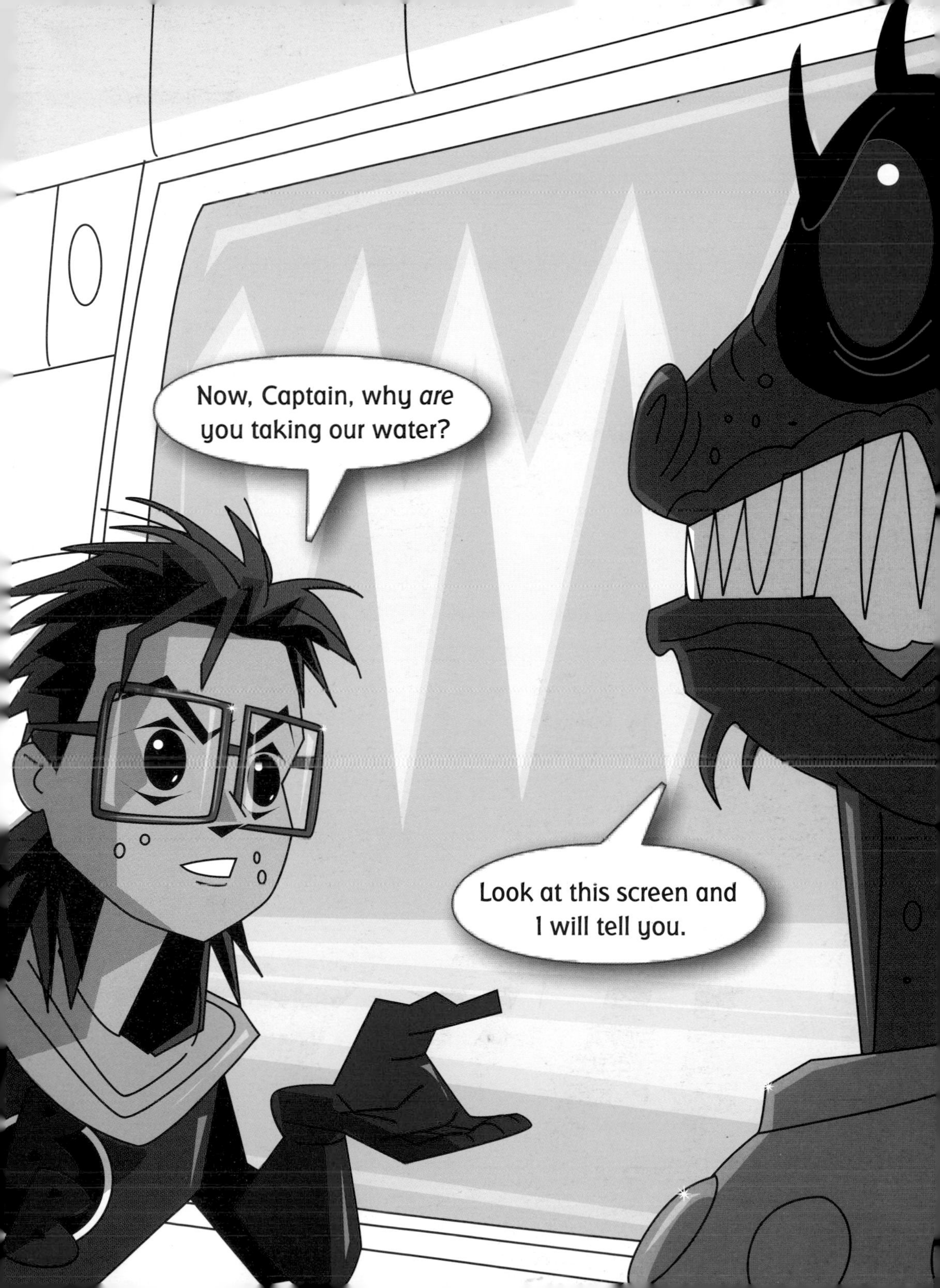
Now, Captain, why *are* you taking our water?
Look at this screen and I will tell you.

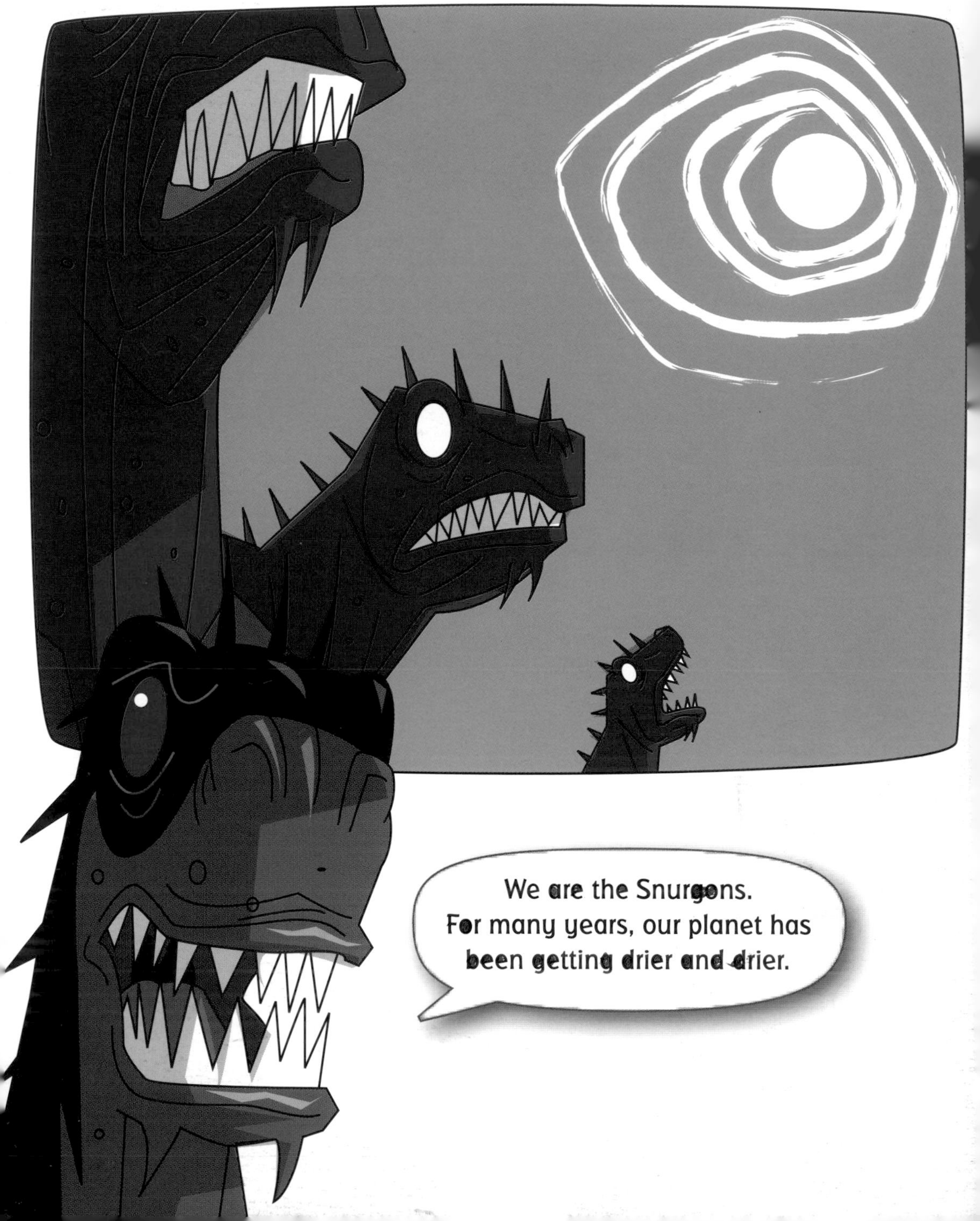
We are the Snurgons.
For many years, our planet has been getting drier and drier.

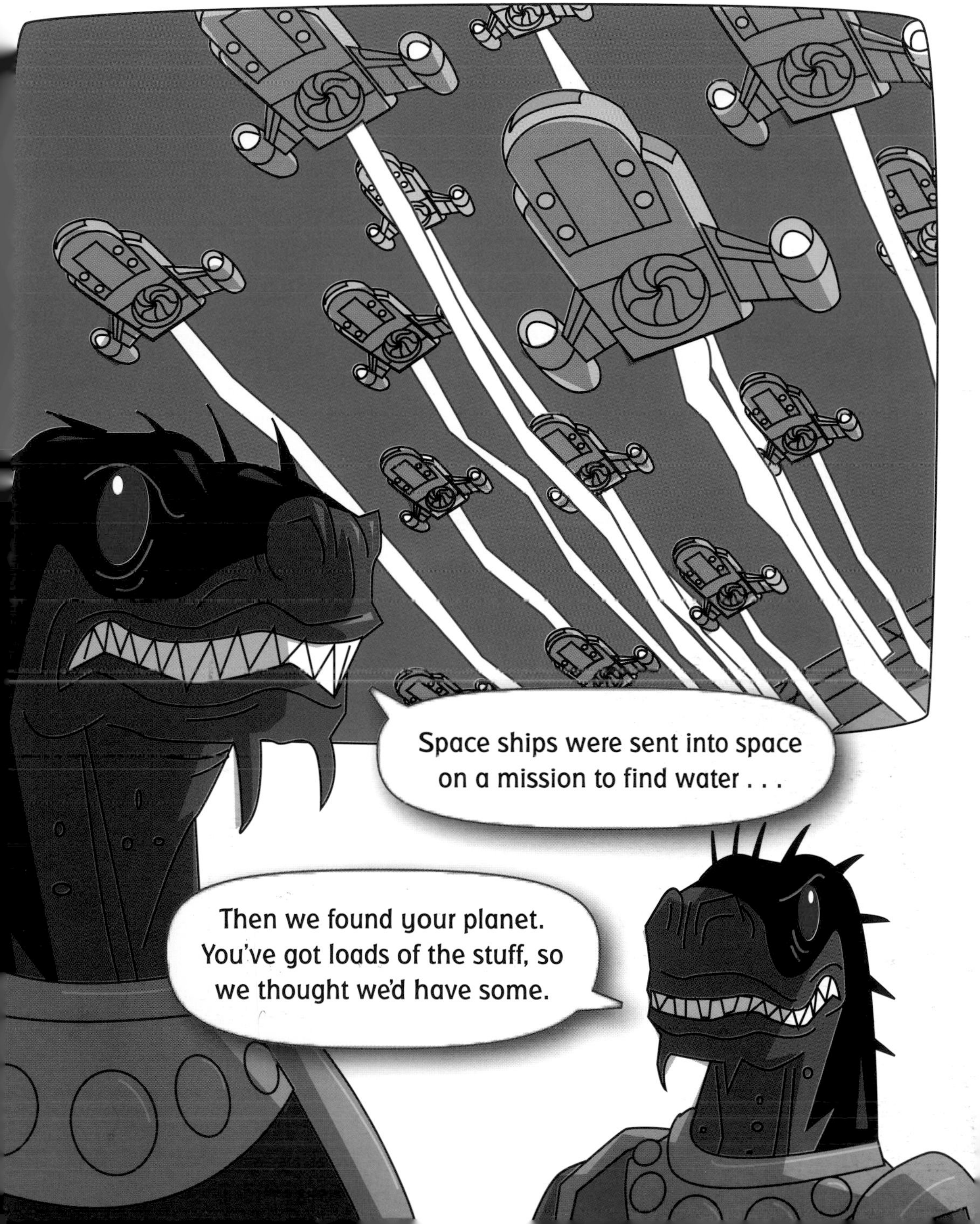
Space ships were sent into space on a mission to find water . . .
Then we found your planet. You've got loads of the stuff, so we thought we'd have some.

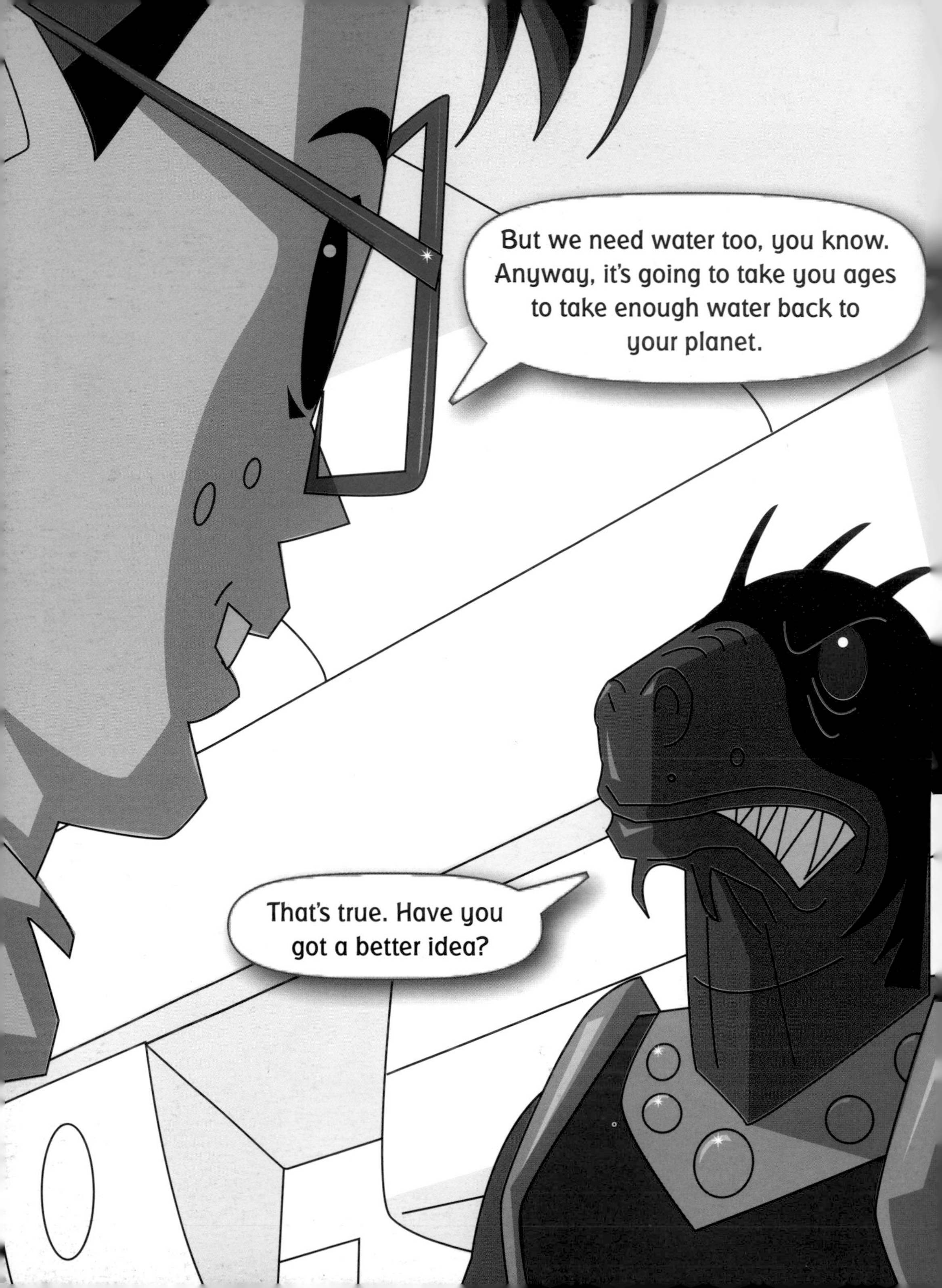
But we need water too, you know. Anyway, it's going to take you ages to take enough water back to your planet.
That's true. Have you got a better idea?

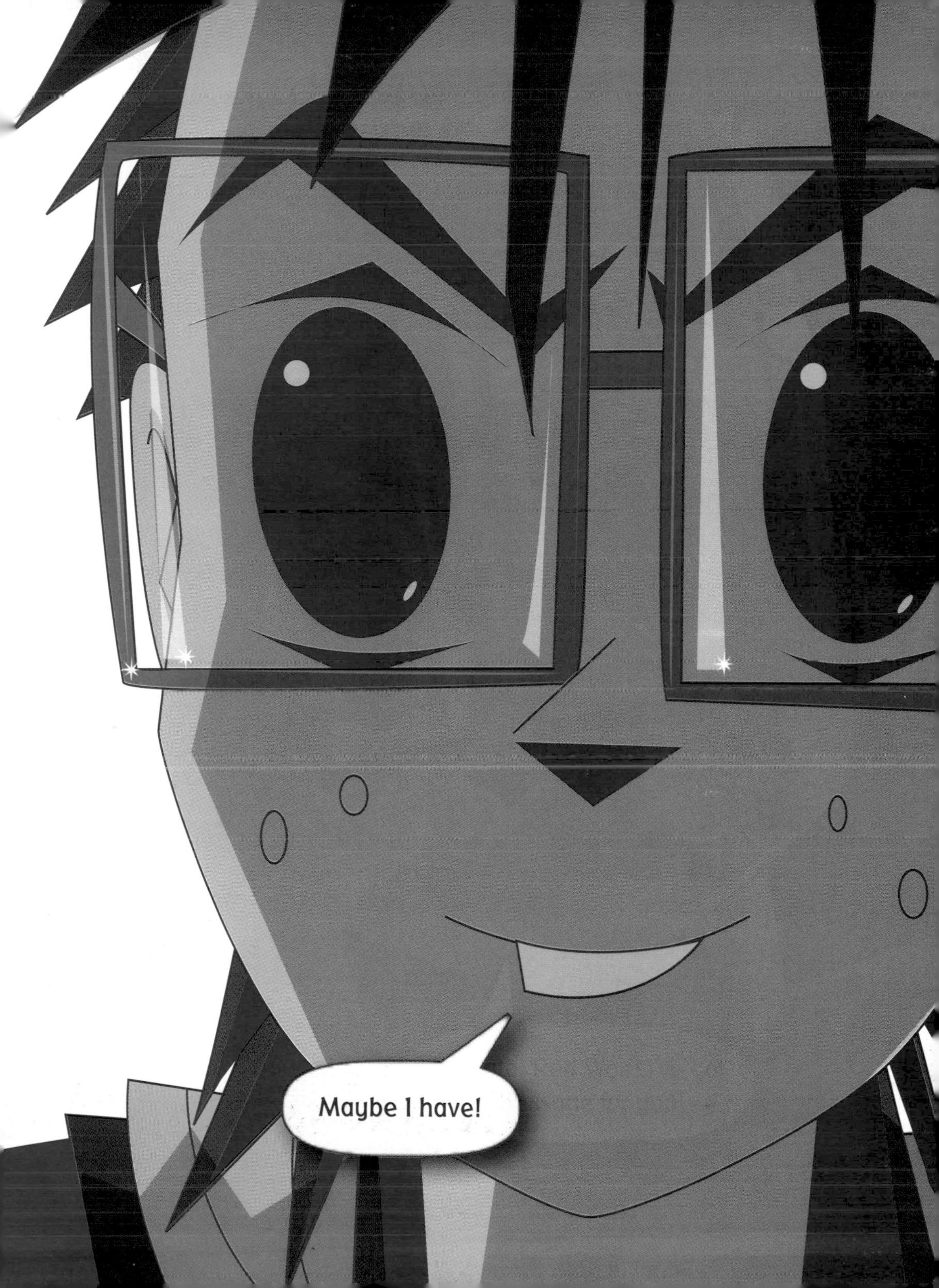
Maybe I have!

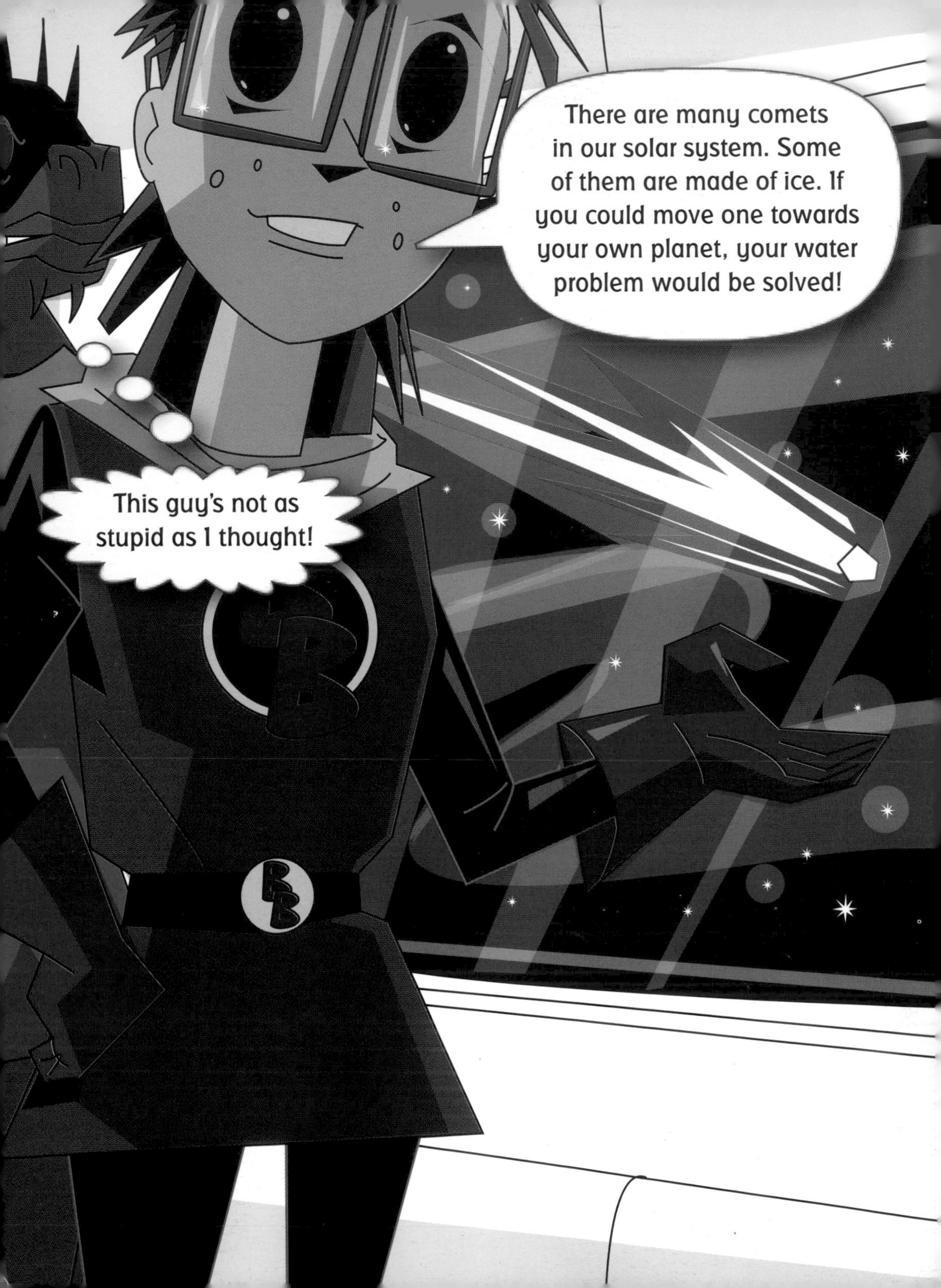
There are many comets in our solar system. Some of them are made of ice. If you could move one towards your own planet, your water problem would be solved!
This guy's not as stupid as I thought!

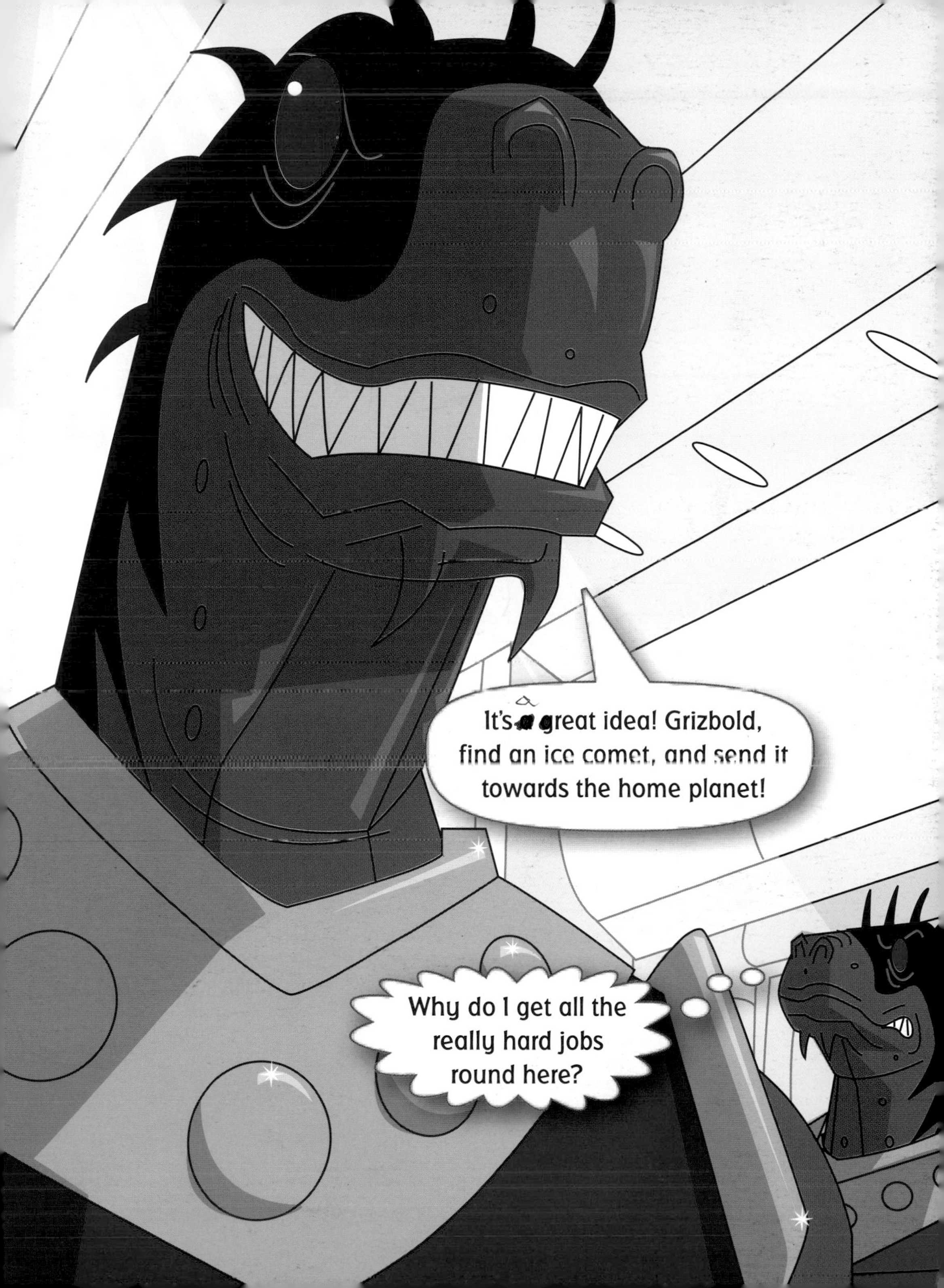

It's a great idea! Grizbold, find an ice comet, and send it towards the home planet!
Why do I get all the really hard jobs round here?

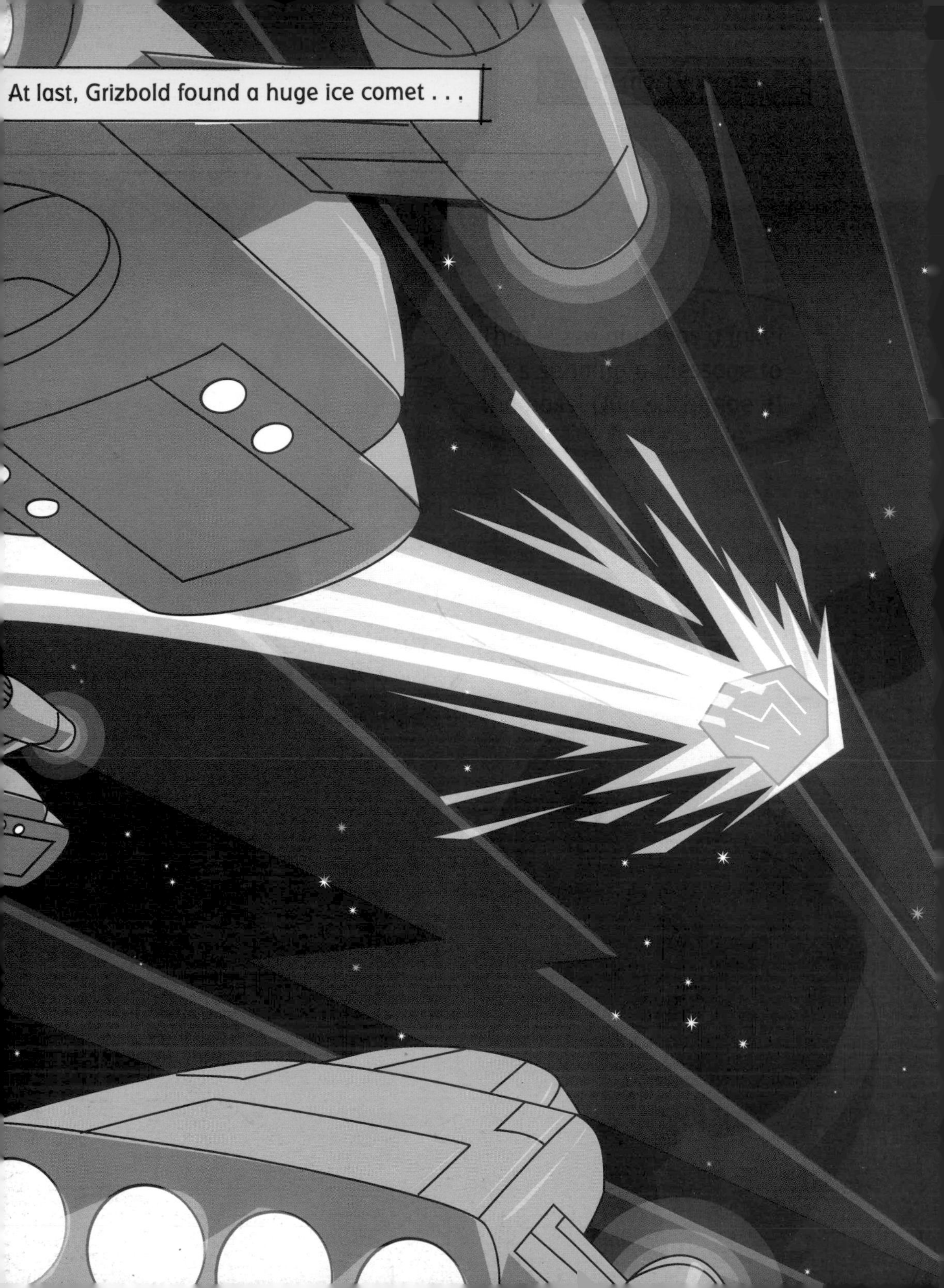
At last, Grizbold found a huge ice comet . . .

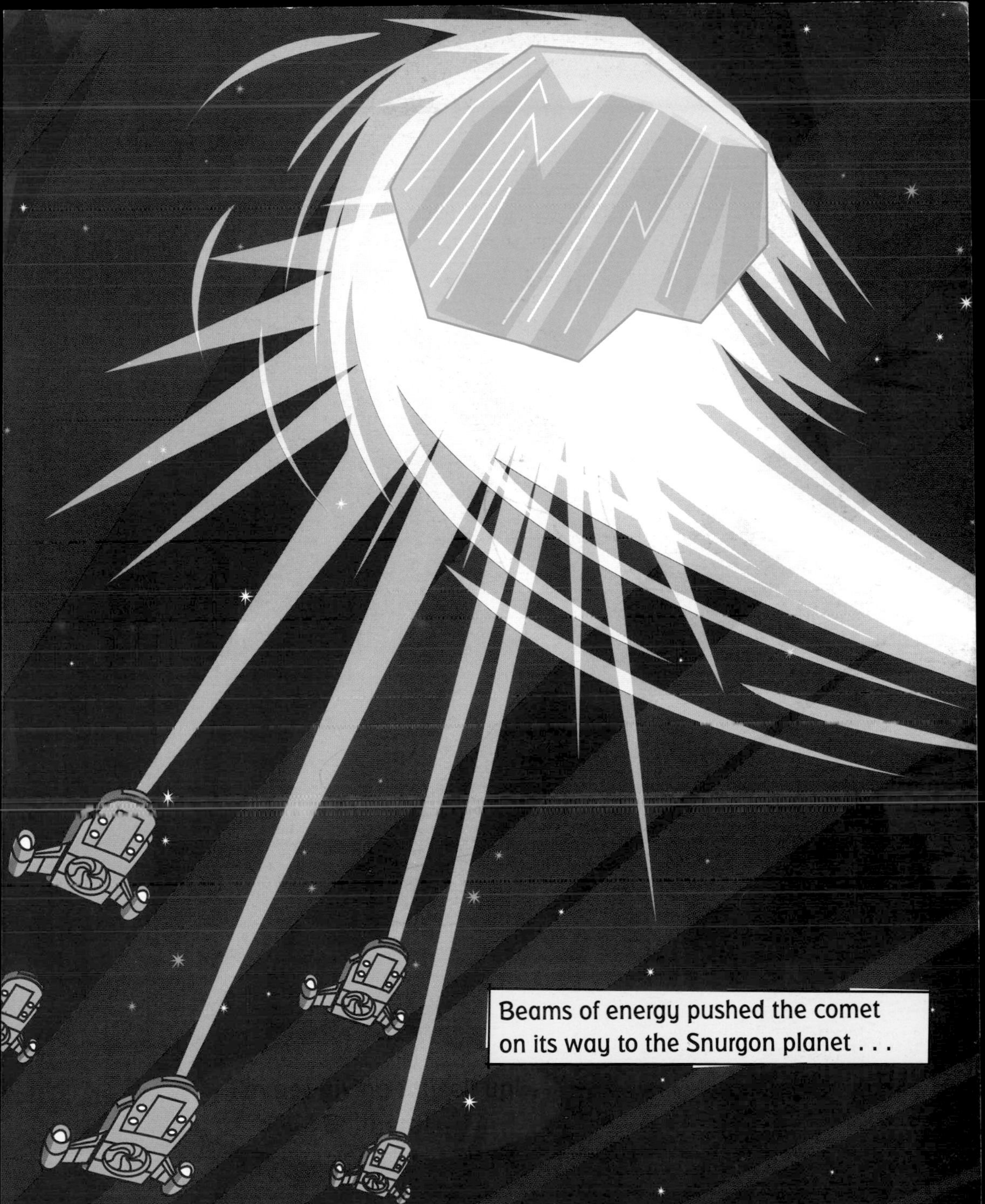
Beams of energy pushed the comet on its way to the Snurgon planet . . .

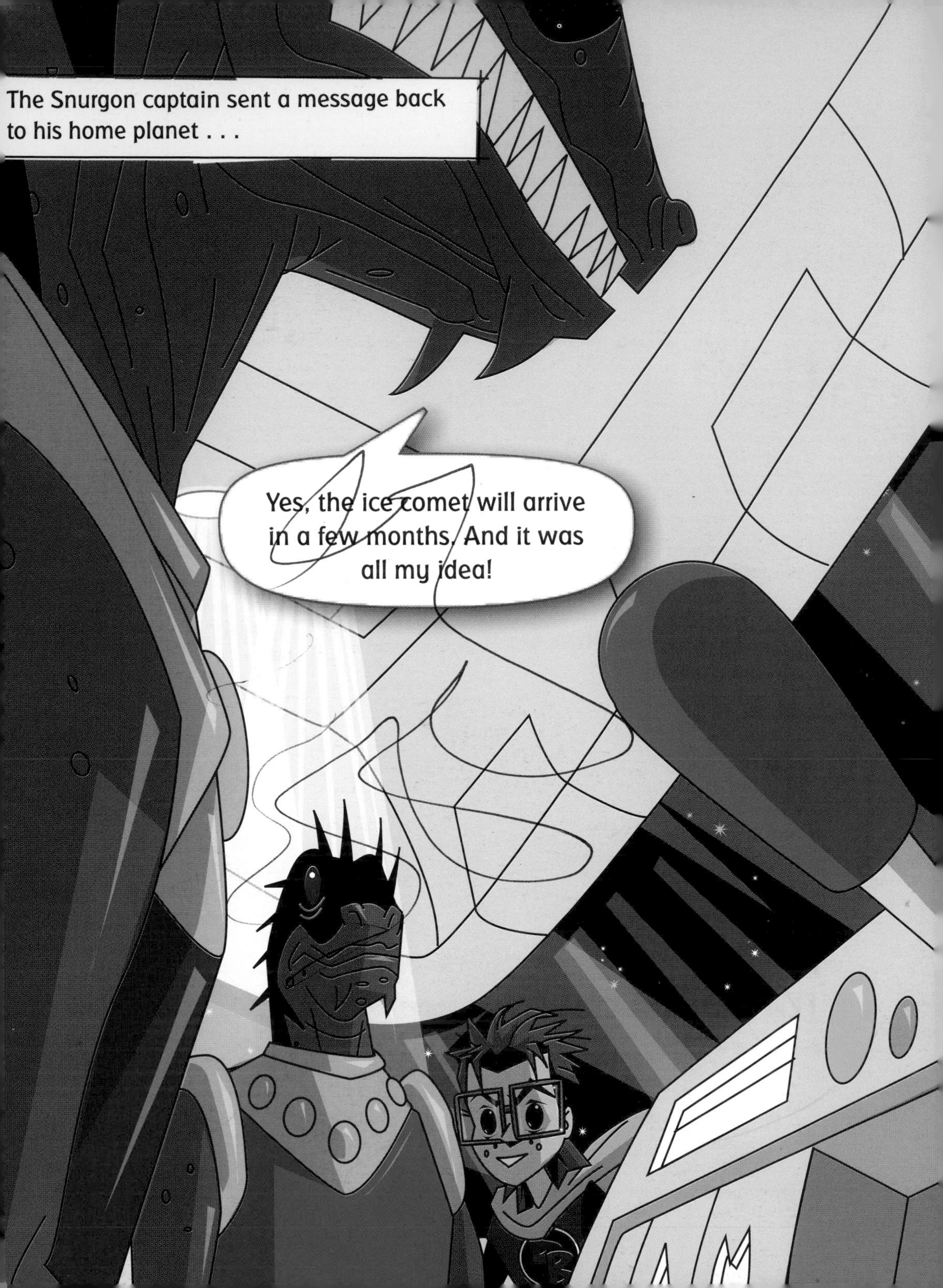
The Snurgon captain sent a message back to his home planet . . .
Yes, the ice comet will arrive in a few months. And it was all my idea!

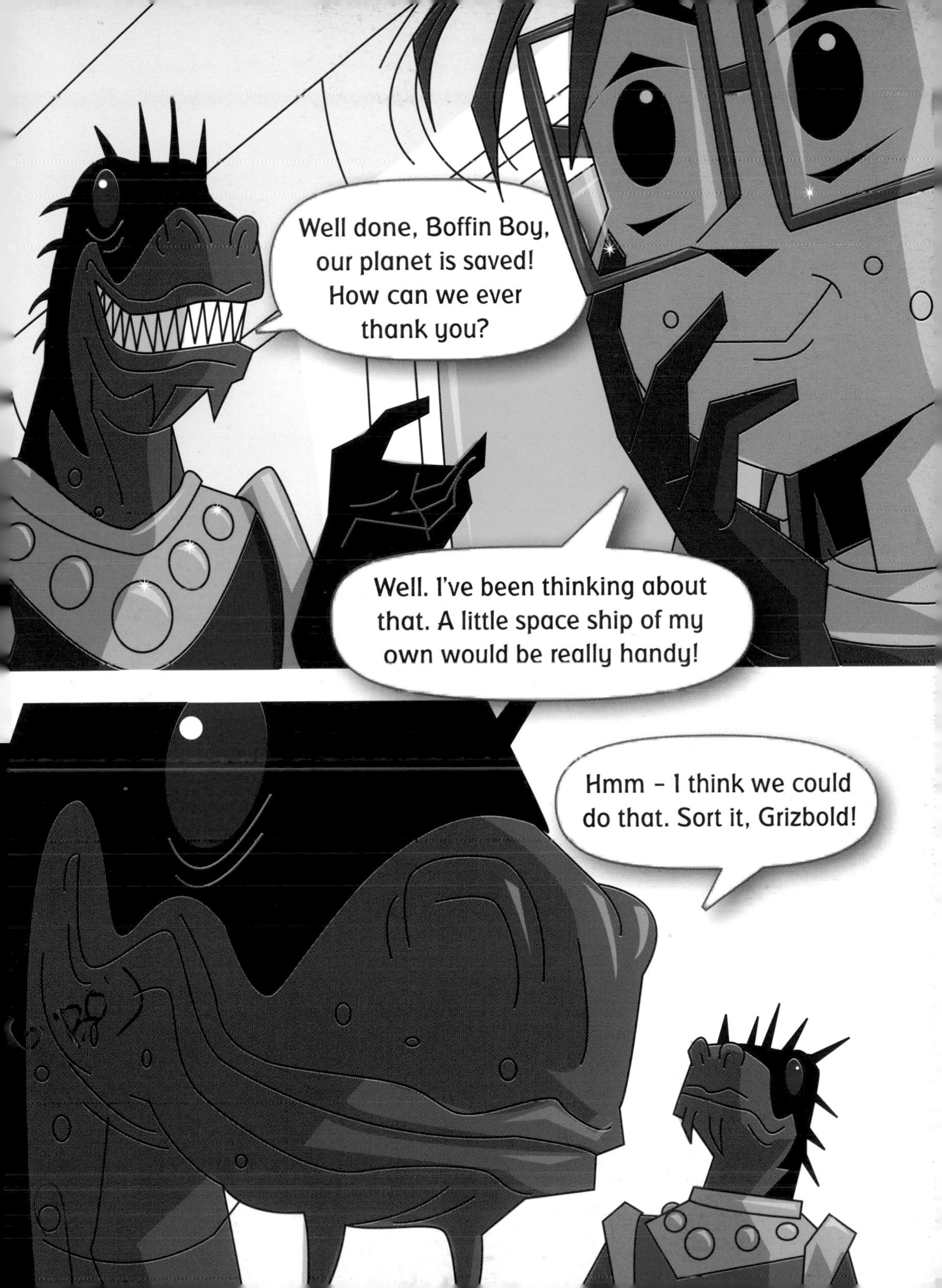
Well done, Boffin Boy, our planet is saved! How can we ever thank you?
Well. I've been thinking about that. A little space ship of my own would be really handy!
Hmm – I think we could do that. Sort it, Grizbold!

Boffin Boy returns to Earth in his new space ship . . .

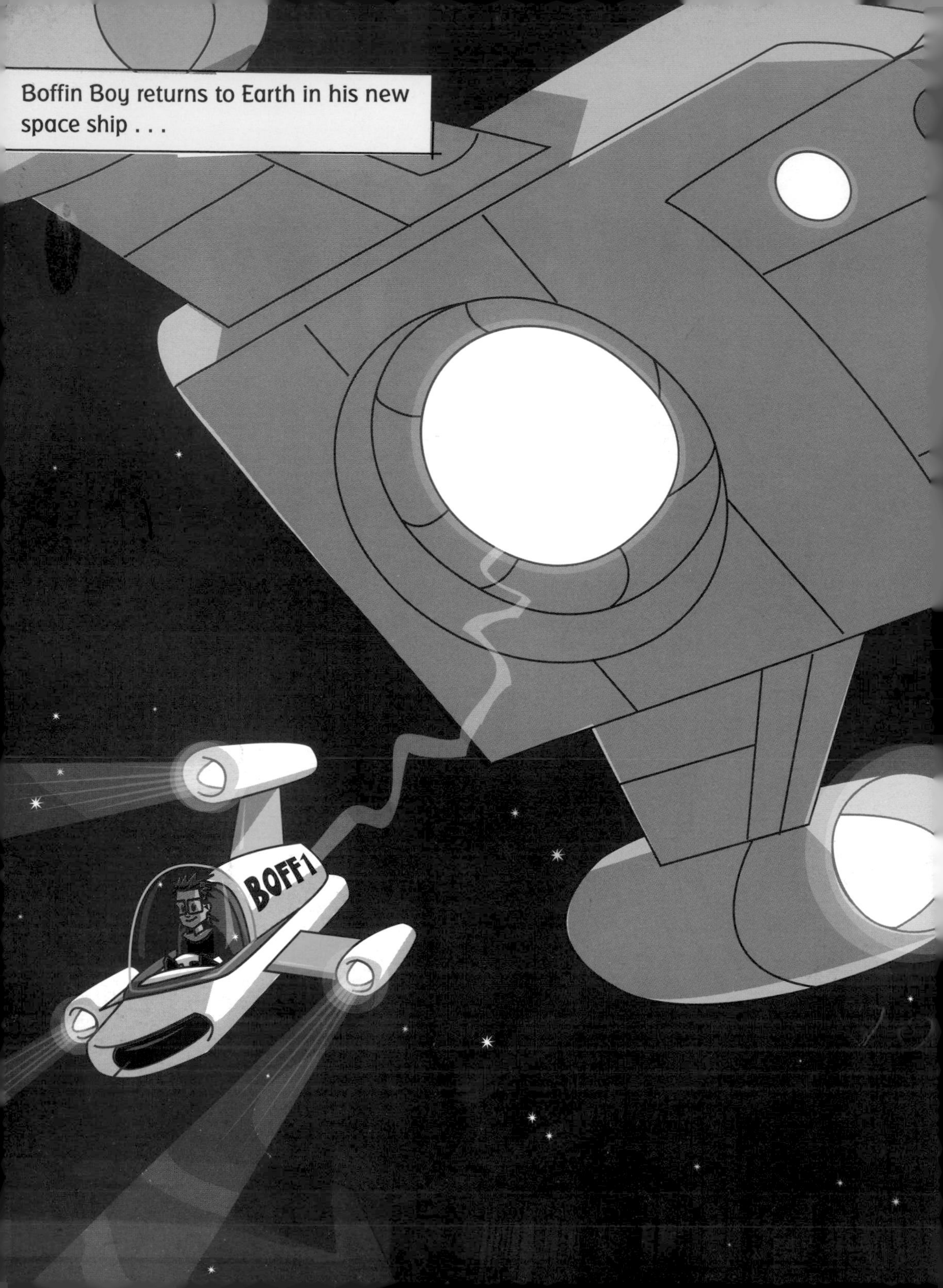
BOFF1

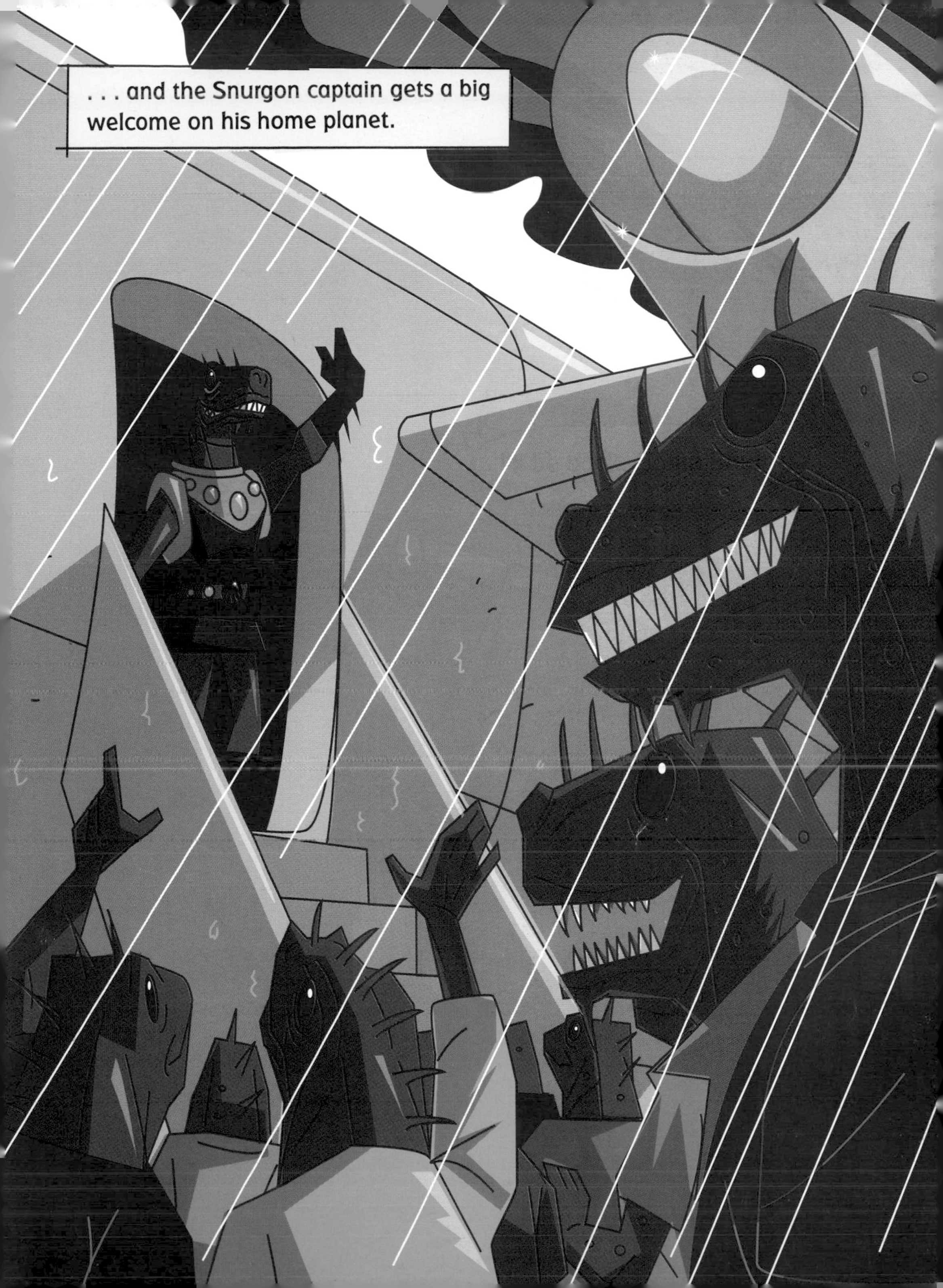
. . . and the Snurgon captain gets a big welcome on his home planet.

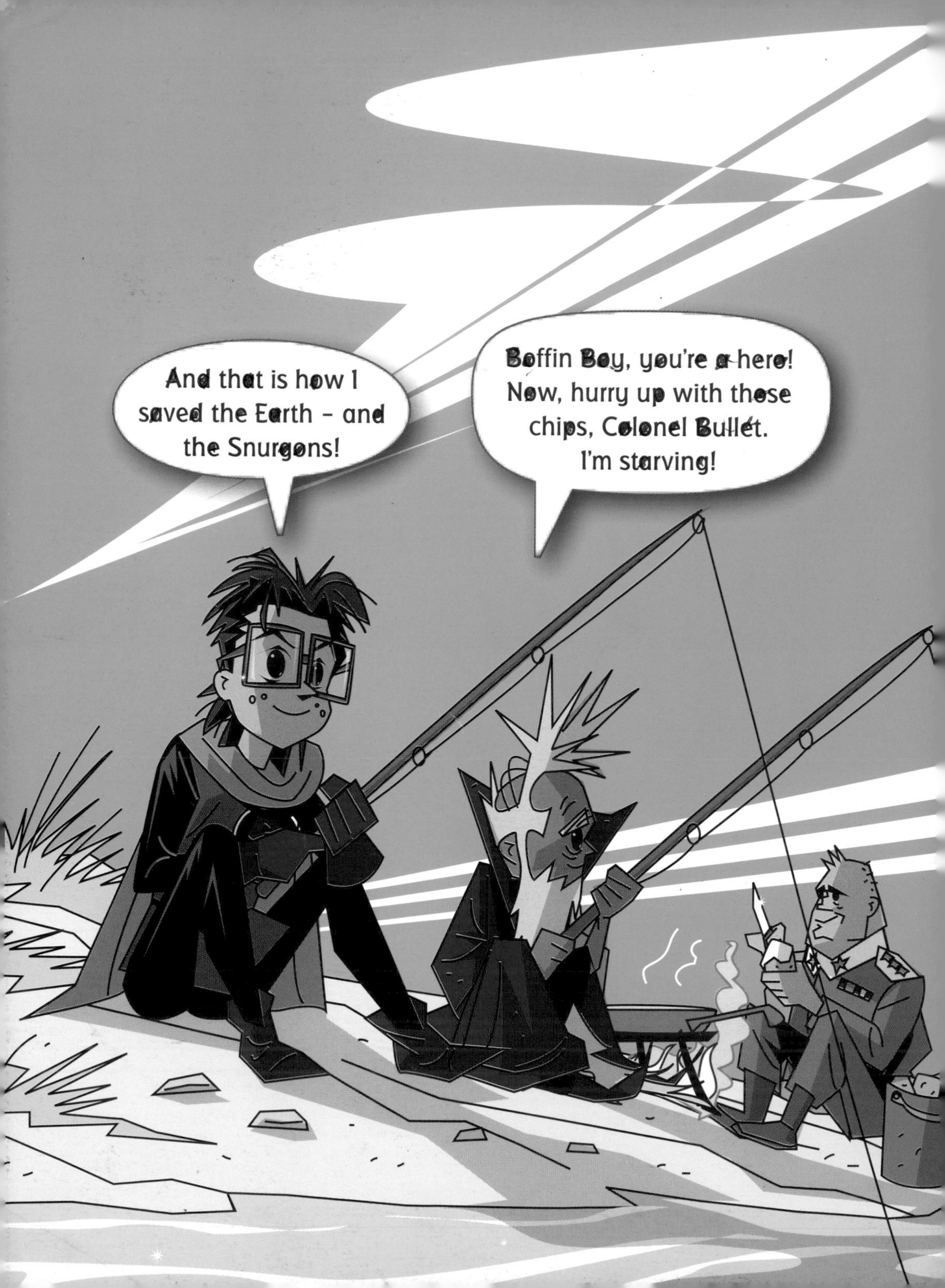
And that is how I saved the Earth – and the Snurgons!
Boffin Boy, you're a hero! Now, hurry up with those chips, Colonel Bullet. I'm starving!

ABOUT THE AUTHOR

David Orme has written over 200 books including poetry collections, fiction and non-fiction, and school text books. When he is not writing books he travels around the country, giving performances, running writing workshops and running courses.

Find out more at:
www.magic-nation.com.

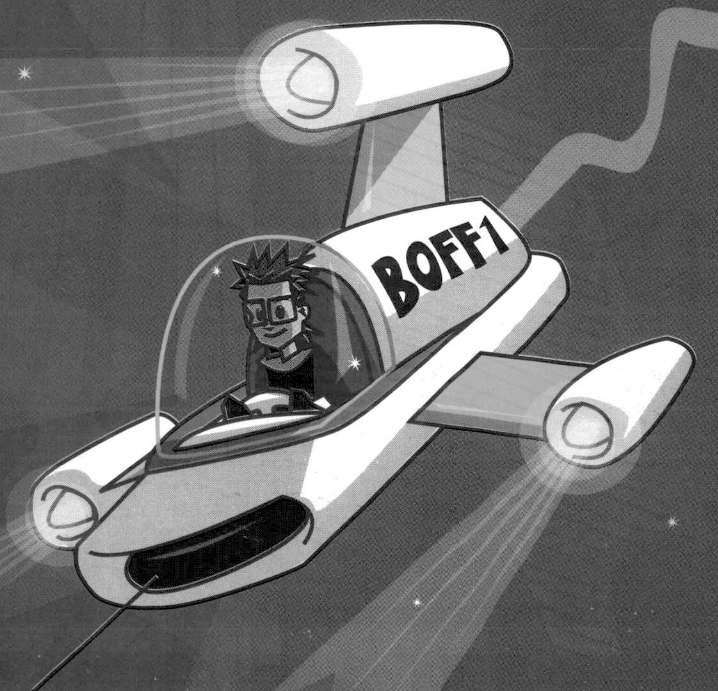
BOFF1